In My Secret Life

A novel
by Amy Bleu

"Edgy and intimate, a seductive read you won't put down."

—**Monica Drake**, author of *Clown Girl*

"A clear-eyed view of the ways people protect themselves in layers and layers of narratives in order to survive the day. Painted without judgment (gratefully), these characters feel like they have something to teach the reader about the realities of daily life as much as they have something to learn. A very engaging read even for prudes and wallflowers—maybe even especially so."

—**Nick Jaina**, author of *Hitomi*

"Bleu is a fierce, uncompromising voice for a new era of radical, surprising and exciting literature."

—**Laura LeMoon**, author of *Dirty*, poet and journalist

IN MY SECRET LIFE

Amy Bleu

Woodhall Press
Norwalk, CT

woodhall press

Woodhall Press, 81 Old Saugatuck Road, Norwalk, CT 06855

WoodhallPress.com

Cover Design: Andrea Faith
Layout Artist: Zoey Moyal

Library of Congress Cataloging-in-Publication Data available

ISBN 978-1-954907-36-2 (paper: alk paper)
ISBN 978-1-954907-37-9 (electronic)

First Edition

Distributed by Independent Publishers Group

(800) 888-4741

Printed in the United States of America

This is a work of fiction. Names, characters, business, events and incidents are the products of the author's imagination. Any resemblance to actual persons, living or dead, or actual events is purely coincidental.

For Kim Dralle, my Kimsperation, and for my first readers, Rachel Chuganey, Jennifer Graham, Krista Nolen, and Kimberly Neal, my Kimpossible. This book would not be possible without any of you.

1. October 9

Take your pill, and everything will be all right. That line always reminded Amelia of herself. She had, as the song said, that super-pale skin and those soft green eyes. She didn't, however, need a pill to make her feel better about life in general, or even an antianxiety med for the flight she would soon board. Instead, she was preparing to take molly before she took off. Amelia figured if she timed it just right, it wouldn't kick in until after she cleared security; it would probably start to hit her while boarding the aircraft. She was very familiar with the drug, well-acquainted with its ways. One pill had a shelf life of about six hours, including the last two hours spent coming down. On such a short flight, Amelia expected to be flying high for four hours, long after the plane had landed.

Amelia was headed to Reno. The flight took only an hour and a half, sometimes less. She was traveling there from her native Portland. She took the light-rail train from downtown, pill in her pocket. Her hand slid inside her pocket every now and then, fingered the pill. Her heart raced every time she touched it. The ring with the amethyst stone, as well as the hematite one, both slid down every time she reached inside, threatening to abandon her bony fingers. Amelia's busy schedule meant she sometimes forgot to eat. Other times, she ingested things like molly or coke instead of food, which robbed her of her appetite for a couple of days. Even if she tried, Amelia wondered if she could maintain a normal weight on her thin frame.

When the light-rail train arrived at Portland International Airport, Amelia took a deep breath. Her heart raced. *There is no turning back once you do this,* she warned herself. *Oh well. Down the hatch.* She opened her mouth and threw the pill in, swallowed quickly and chased it with a swig of water. She grabbed her bags and pulled them off the train. Her ticket was on her phone, and she had already checked in on the app, so she removed her ID from her wallet and dumped the remainder of her water bottle at the liquid disposal station by the security check.

Standing in line, she fiddled with her ID card and her phone. *What if my pill hasn't dissolved, and the body scan shows it going down my throat?* she wondered. *Will they tell me I can't board?* She chided herself for having such a foolish idea. She felt her stomach begin to knot as the first rush of cold hit her blood. She was definitely on her way somewhere. She bit her lip and wished the line would move more quickly. Amelia was sure her pupils were beginning to dilate. *Will the TSA let me through if I look like an ecstasy monster?* she thought. She felt jittery and struggled to center herself in the line. She took off her shoes and sent them down the belt, then went through the body scan. The TSA agent looked at her and then looked at the small screen behind her, waiting for a signal. Amelia turned and saw the screen turn green with the word "OK" illuminated in the middle. "OK," the TSA agent repeated.

Amelia went to the belt, grabbed her shoes and her bags. Her vision started to swirl a bit. She remembered that she had no more water in her bottle, and dug around inside the purse next to the bottle to find that she also had no gum. *Party necessities.* She went to the newsstand and found both. She was so shaky now and wide-eyed that she feared the cashier wouldn't sell her anything and would call security to ensure that she wouldn't be let on any flights. *Relax!* another part of her brain said. *This woman is busy working and doesn't give a shit what you're doing.* The woman counted back Amelia's change, dropped it into her sweaty palm, and gave her a plastic smile as she said good-bye. The cashier's eyes followed her as she backed away from the counter.

Over the loudspeaker, she heard the boarding call for her flight. Amelia raced to the gate and waited until they were boarding her section. She stood in line and popped a piece of gum into her mouth. Her jaw had already begun to clench and was now feeling relieved. People ahead of her in line began to move, so she floated forward thoughtlessly. Her little fuzzy pink neck pillow was sticking out of her purse. Her fingers ached to rub it. She ran her fingers along the hem of her sweater instead. Why did soft fabric feel so good to touch? When it was her turn to present her ticket, the man at the gate stared blankly at Amelia and said, "Just a moment, please." *Oh god, he can tell that I'm high. He's not going to let me on.* He ran into the jet bridge and then ran back out a few seconds later. "Sorry," he said, scanning her e-ticket, "someone shut the other door inside of there and forgot to open it again. We want to make sure you get in and get cozy."

Her nervous smile dripping off her lips, she oozed down the jet bridge and rolled onto the aircraft. She had trouble making sense of seat assignments but eventually found her seat and threw her suitcase into the overhead bin. She took out her gum, water, headphones, and pillow, and then stowed her large handbag snugly under the seat in front of her. She heaved a sigh of relief, put her headphones on, and wrapped the furry pillow around her neck. The music and the soft fur enhanced the warm, fuzzy tingling inside of her heart and her belly. She tried to keep the sky in view as the plane took off, but the air kept swirling.

A woman was seated two seats down from her, and there was an empty seat in the middle. Amelia thought the woman seated near her looked nice. *Don't you fucking talk to her,* she warned herself. Talking felt so good on molly! Talking and listening! *Well, you can listen to Sam,* she reasoned with herself, *when you get off the plane.* She didn't remember having any more thoughts until some turbulence hit. The plane was rattling around in the sky and she was thinking, *Whee, this is so much fun!* But a voice deeper down inside her brain said, *You used to be scared when this happened. This might be an indicator of danger.* Amelia shook off the second voice and went back into her reverie. The plane landed suddenly. It seemed that only five minutes had passed since takeoff.

Amelia had been sure that, since she would be peaking on the plane, off only one hit, she'd be able to pass for sober when she landed. She couldn't get anything in her line of sight to stay still; it all spun like she was on a carousel. Her stomach felt tight as her heart swooned over every sensation. *Run your fingers through your hair: miniature orgasm.* She grabbed her phone out of her pocket and texted Sam. She had a sudden burst of inspiration, told him that she had been nervous to fly and had taken an antianxiety pill. If she seemed loopy, she explained, that would be why.

The other passengers made their way off the plane and into the airport and Amelia glided down the aisle behind everyone. She hoped there would be time for a cigarette. *That first cigarette after you come up on molly is the best,* she recalled. Sam texted that he would be there in about five minutes. *Perfect,* she said to herself, exiting the airport toward the smoking area. She sat down in the smoking section and lit up. She inhaled the cigarette and relished the feeling every time the smoke filled her lungs. Music from her flight playlist was vibrating inside her ears.

A man pulled up in a white car. Amelia had never met him before, but he waved in recognition from inside the car. She vaguely remembered sending him pictures of herself when she had applied for the gig. Still, she felt timid, never having seen his picture or knowing quite how he might look. Her friend Emma had referred her to him, had given her his email address, and had only told her that Sam was relatively young. She called him the Reno Guy. She and Amelia had names for all their photographers, but most of them were based less on geography and had more to do with their kinks: the Edger, the Diaper Guy. Sometimes it was taken from their screen name on their online portfolio: Dark Montana, Nefarious Shadows.

After Amelia went to the hotel with Sam and had quick, vanilla sex, she understood why he was known (and would always be known) only as the Reno Guy.

The sex was a blur but Amelia could at least recall the next day that it had been brief and that nothing kinky had been involved. She had never had sex with a man for money before. Amelia was a model who worked in many genres: fashion, glamour, art, fetish, and pinup. Recently she had begun to take on a little "porna." Porna, she had been told, was a term used to describe adult content that was geared toward women, and Amelia was passionate about the idea of making videos and posing for photographs that showcased real female sexuality. For that reason, she had no problem showing the camera how she jerked off, or how she could make a girlfriend come. She enjoyed being with women as much as she did men, but the outside package of a woman usually got her going more than a man. In order for her to get into a man, she really had to get to know him, which was why she typically shunned the idea of fucking some random guy for the going rate (two to three hundred per hour, for a pro-amateur like Amelia, or Emma).

Emma was less discriminating. She had been doing it for so long, and two hundred dollars was two hundred dollars, in her mind. If she had to lie on her back all day, making two hundred dollars every hour, well… that kind of money does add up. She still did regular modeling jobs sometimes, too, but, as she had told Amelia when she was pitching the idea of her working for Sam: "I prefer having sex to posing in lingerie or naked. I don't have to think of all these different poses and draw it out for hours for a couple of hundred dollars. I can have sex with the photographer, or *fauxtographer*," she explained, making air quotes with her fingers to emphasize the distinction, "and I'll have two hundred dollars in five minutes without expending nearly as much energy!"

Amelia was happy for her friend, if she didn't like modeling as much and was able to do what she really enjoyed: making money quickly. But she wondered if Emma still enjoyed having sex. Emma always talked about it with a cool distance, and reveled in her ability to get guys off quickly. Amelia didn't want to be desensitized to the touch of a lover. She sensed that being a sex worker for years had changed Emma's relationship with her own body, that she somehow might not feel like her body belonged to herself anymore. She had played lookout once for Emma on their first trip to New York together, when Emma was sleeping with a man after he'd photographed her and Amelia together. The man was moaning while he had sex with Emma, as she was lying silent and motionless on the bed. "Can I come in your mouth?" he asked in between gasps.

"Oh, yeah, I don't care," Emma mumbled. He extricated himself and then began thrusting in and out of her mouth. Amelia was holding his camera for him. She peered through the lens and felt simultaneously intrigued and repulsed. The man who was fucking her friend in their shared hotel room in Manhattan was a senior, slim but with an old man's saggy gut. He pulled himself out of Emma's mouth and she held it open. Amelia was fascinated. How could her friend stand being with that dirty old man? How could this guy not notice how disinterested her friend appeared?

Sam turned out to be forty, but Amelia initially thought he was thirty. That would have been just five years younger than she herself was. She was glad to get a young guy for her first, and a generous one, who had offered to pay well above the standard rate. He wasn't attractive, but he wasn't ugly. He was simply average, except in his shorts: his member was a dwarf. Two inches, maybe, when he was rock hard. Amelia would have felt strange trying to feign interest, had she not been on molly. With the drug in her veins, making everything erotic, Amelia was able to enjoy herself, to some degree. Sam's video camera was set up on top of a dresser, since he had forgotten his tripod, and it captured every move they made together. She didn't orgasm but she felt almost as happy as she would have if she had been cuddling with one of her friends back home on MDMA. It felt innocuous.

Sam showered after he finished and Amelia stayed in bed, curled up inside the sheets, with her vision still swimming. For some reason, she had always wanted to find herself in this kind of situation: lying in a hotel bed having just been fucked by a stranger for a thousand dollars. So, even though the actual sex hadn't done anything for her, she felt turned on just by lying in bed, thinking of herself as a dirty whore. She couldn't wait for Sam to leave so that she could jerk off.

After he left, she obliged herself by taking the vibrator out. When she finished getting herself off, she climbed out of bed in search of a cigarette. She opened the door gingerly and stepped out into the quiet night. There was a "no smoking" sign outside of her door, so she headed down the stairs and walked around the property until she found a smoking area. Euphoria and wonder still filled her, and she was energized by the cigarette smoke. But she found herself struggling to think clearly, after putting out the cigarette, and walking back toward the stairwell, she realized that her key didn't say her room number and that she'd forgotten to look at which room she was even staying in. That was a first for her, getting lost at a hotel. She wandered the halls, hoping that she would eventually intuit which room was hers. Rounding a corner, she ambled through an open door. *There it is! The ice maker!* Somehow she thought it was what she had been looking for all along, and she pulled a cube of ice out of the machine, plopped down on the ground and sucked on it. The wet, cold feeling of the ice moved through her entire body in the most exhilarating way. But something in one of the corners of her mind interrupted obnoxiously: *I think you were actually looking for something else.*

My room! Amelia stood up and began to roam the halls some more. She waited until she approached a door and got a sense that it might lead to her room. With trepidation, she inserted the key and saw the light above the lock turn an affirming green.

Amelia shook her head in wonder, shocked that she had found her room on the first try. *Well, besides that brief sojourn in the ice room.* She knew that she would have to come down from the drug eventually, so she walked into the bathroom and drew herself a bath, figuring it would ease the comedown. She really needed a bowl of weed for that, but that wasn't something she was willing to risk sneaking onto the plane. Amelia didn't even really smoke pot very much, but she loved it on a molly come down.

As she became more sober, and more tired, the bath grew colder, so Amelia climbed out and toweled off. She was clumsy and bumping into the bathroom counter and the door frame as she headed back to the bedroom. Her mind and body felt so sensitive to everything. The warm and fuzzy feeling of the high had transformed into a nasty hangover, one that made nearly everything feel harsh to her skin, in stark contrast to how pleasing every sensation had been just an hour earlier. She tumbled into bed and fell into a long, uninterrupted sleep. She woke up ten hours later, dehydrated from the molly, her forehead mysteriously freckled with hives.

The events of the evening prior had left her tired and slow to realize that she was having an allergic reaction to something. She had nothing unusual in the room. It must have been the goose down pillows! Amelia hadn't known that she had an allergy to goose down. She had never stayed in a nice hotel room until recently, had never had to worry about it. Making a mental note to invest in some allergy medication, Amelia rolled up her ten one-hundred-dollar bills and tucked them in the inside pocket of her purse and zipped it tight. She scanned the room and ascertained that she had left no signs of any illegal activities, so she opened the front door. Suitcase in hand, pounding ache in her head left over from the molly, she slogged off to her next job.

2. October 14

Mia stared out onto the ocean from behind her huge bay window. She and Burton owned their home on the Elliot Bay portion of the Puget Sound. It was usually calm during the vespertine hours, and tonight brought no exception. The fire in their fireplace was equally docile. *Don't they know it's the end of the world?*

Leaping up from the couch, Mia raced down the hallway that led from their living room to their bedroom. She had been pacing all evening. It was uncharacteristic of Burton to be out late without calling or answering his cell phone. Not that he didn't enjoy going out for a drink late after work, but he was always home for a nightcap with his wife, even on the nights when he went out with colleagues or clients for cocktails.

Did Burton drink too much? Perhaps. But he had great taste in wine, scotch, and bourbon. He could drink most of a bottle of red wine and leave Mia with barely a glass, but they both enjoyed a good steak or had lobster while he lapped up all his wine. He seemed too classy to be an alcoholic.

Still, Mia had often begun to tease him about his expanding waistline. "I think you shrunk all my pants!" he had teased her one day. She'd shot back in a loving, playful voice: "No, honey, it's not that your pants are shrinking; it's that you're growing!"

Despite joking about it openly that day, she had a solemn wish for Burton to get serious about his health. A top software engineer, Burton traveled often: conferences in SoCal, Tokyo, Barcelona. He and his wife had traveled to Greece for pleasure, so that Mia could learn more about her heritage, and they'd gone to Italy and France solely because of their reputations for being romantic countries. Burton always preferred to bring Mia and his camera along with him, whether he was traveling for work or for fun. Photography was a passion of his: shooting landscapes, and portraits of his wife. He took pictures of the different skylines of the cities they visited, captured views of downtown areas as seen from boats or bridges.

Mia found that she wasn't always able to accompany Burton on his trips, as she also enjoyed fostering her own career, in catering, which had just begun to thrive. They ate decadent meals and drank the finest wines and liquor every night on their trips, *and why not? It was a vacation, right?* Mia had reasoned with herself. Then one day she realized that if Burton was always traveling, he wasn't just eating and drinking indulgently for a lark: it was his way of life now.

Mia wanted him to be careful with himself and live a long life with her.

Bursting into their bedroom, she scanned the entire area as if it somehow held clues. Nothing was out of the ordinary. A couple of Burton's socks were on the floor, just hadn't made it into the hamper. She always shook her head and sighed before picking them up, baffled as to why he couldn't place them in the hamper himself. Mia had the idea to grab them again, but it was a fleeting impulse that she ignored. There was a storm brewing inside of her, and she knew that, soon, she would never be upset by his socks again.

Mia had been lucky enough to have been married to her soulmate for thirteen years so far. The man looked at her from across the room sometimes with an expression reserved for a new lover: there was something hungry and curious about it. Burton even gazed at her sometimes just before they retired to the bedroom, as they were nestled under throw blankets on their loveseat, as if he was still longing to figure out her body, as if he hadn't already read it like a map and then charted new courses across it all these years.

It's all over now, baby blue, an old song sang inside her mind. Mia never drank alone but she thought that a spill of Burton's scotch might calm her nerves. She poured it neat and drank it as quickly as she could handle, trying to ignore the burn.

Burton would have chided her: "There's no burn! That is a sixty-year-old scotch you've got in your hand, Baby Blue. That is nothing but smooth." Mia remembered being nestled in the crook of his arm, cuddled up on the couch one night, when he was teasing her, calling her Baby Blue. She had asked him why he had always called her that name. "It's your eyes," Burton explained.

"But my eyes are brown!" Mia had protested, giggling.

Burton had paused thoughtfully before responding, unconsciously rubbing the shawl that covered Mia's slender arm. "It isn't the color: it's something behind them. Not depression or anything maudlin; just something ... *deep.*"

I am *blue, Burton,* she thought now, looking out at the ocean again. *Deep as the water.*

She remembered a poem she'd read several years earlier: *Yo En El Fondo Del Mar,* by Alfonsina Stroni.

Me, at the bottom of the sea. That was what it meant. Mia shivered. *We won't go that deep,* she warned herself. The poet had killed herself by walking out into the ocean until she had drowned.

The scotch had eased Mia's anxiety, but she was left with a profound swell of sadness so intense that she feared she might soon go numb in order to avoid the weight of everything crashing down upon her.

The doorbell rang. She wasn't shaking any longer: she was resigned. *Burton wouldn't ring the doorbell,* she said to herself. *You already know who it is.*

Two officers stood on the front porch, just like in the movies. Mia didn't register anything they said for a whole minute, except she was able to make out the words "car accident."

3. October 14

Over the years, Amelia had been able to work with Burton Hughes only about once every other season—far fewer times a year than she worked with most of her regulars. Burton shot so many models, and apologized frequently for not being able to book her more often, but Amelia understood: why wouldn't everyone want to work with him? His photographs were gorgeous: lush with color, shade, and depth, imbued with feeling. Burton could take what he was feeling and get a model somehow to convey it.

Amelia took the city bus from the hotel she had slept at, near the Seattle airport, to the studio that Burton had leased for the occasion. It was just north of the city center. Burton greeted her at the front door. She rolled her suitcase in as he held the door open and asked her about her trip. She told him that it had been fine, and she inquired about all the traveling that she had seen him doing recently, according to Facebook. He laughed, and responded, "Well, I didn't know that a passport could become invalid before its expiration date, if it has too many stamps and there isn't room for any more!" He laughed again, good-naturedly, and Amelia giggled and shook her head.

Burton had her pose in her favorite fashions, and then lingerie. Finally he asked her to pose nude and she was happy to stand naked near the white backdrop and let Burton color her in.

Amelia asked Burton more questions about his vacations, and where he would go next. He talked at great length about the next one he and his wife had planned. "We've never been to Iceland and she's never been to Ireland, so I said 'what the heck, let's do both!'" he roared.

"Wow," Amelia marveled, "that's so great!" She couldn't wait until she could afford to travel outside of the country and get away for pleasure rather than business. She pictured herself on a tropical island, where she might learn to speak a foreign language, sparsely but with ease, at least well enough to ask for directions, order drinks, and be polite. She imagined that she would be surrounded by lush green leaves and bright blue ocean waters.

Looking through his viewfinder, Burton nodded confidently and said, "I think we've got them all." He began to tear down one of his lights.

After all his gear and Amelia's clothing were safely packed up, Burton did something he had never done with Amelia before. He had been generous in offering her rides to the next shoot or her hotel room in the past, but this time he asked if she might like to have a drink and some lunch at a bar with him before he dropped her off at her next assignment.

Amelia would be shooting something more erotic, with her friend Natalia, at a photographer's home next. *One drink,* she reasoned, *couldn't hurt.*

Tacos and tequila were the special of the day at El Borracho. Burton had suggested going there, calling it his favorite taqueria. Amelia had never met a taco she didn't like, and she had recently begun to cultivate a taste for tequila, enjoying the spirited, energetic sort of buzz she incurred when she imbibed it. They sped through Seattle in Burton's Lexus until they reached First Avenue.

El Borracho was just outside of the Pike Place Market. Amelia had always had an affinity for the market, despite shying away from other tourist hubs. The smell of fish in the air never bothered her, even after she became vegan. *The air is full of fish and mystery.* The old Ani DiFranco lyric came to her as she made her way past the market with Burton, walking to El Borracho from where he had parked the car. The sky above began to fill with clouds, pregnant with raindrops, cloaked in gray.

Amelia had grown up in Tacoma, where the paper mills stunk up the air. Seattle's smelly little sister, Tacoma was not quite punk rock enough to be Olympia. She recalled taking the bus to Seattle with her mother when she was young, just for a day trip. Around the first of each month, they would hit the market for her mother's fish, veggies, fruit, and fresh pasta, and then Amelia was always allowed to pick out a handful of candy. Amelia favored the chocolate-covered cherries or dried fruit logs covered in coconut shavings. If her mother had enough money left over, they could have lunch down on the pier: fried fish and chips, or clam chowder.

Burton held the door open and Amelia walked into the restaurant. She was surprised at how common it was; it was sort of a dive. That kind of environment never bothered Amelia, but she could tell from Burton's style (his expensive haircut, his polo shirts and Ray-Ban sunglasses, the way he carried himself—not to mention the pictures of food that he posted on his Instagram) that he had more refined tastes. She wondered what had driven him to choose this simple joint, but she didn't mind; they had a vast array of vegan options on the menu for her to choose from.

Amelia thought she would probably look slimmer in her next set of photos if she ordered a salad, but then she shrugged off the insecurity. Besides, she couldn't seem to find a salad option on the menu. *It's not like anyone will ever see these photos anyway*, she reminded herself. *Only Hector's vaults.* She decided to splurge and order the vegan tacos. She shook her head at herself, wondering when she would ever relax and let go a little more. *Oh well.* Tacos before a shoot was a step in the right direction. She ordered two and Burton ordered three. There was a pineapple jalapeno margarita on the menu, which sounded enticing to Amelia, so she decided to take her tequila that way.

Amelia and Burton discussed the world of freelance photography. Burton revealed he was self-conscious about not wanting to be branded as an amateur. "Not a chance," Amelia said sincerely, and raised her margarita.

"Cheers," he responded with a coy smile, touching his glass to hers. She explained to him why she admired his work so much: the lighting, the attention to detail during editing, the way he plotted his moves and pointed the camera, hitting Amelia from the right angles.

Burton blushed and disappeared inside his drink. After his long sip, he told her, "I've been submitting pieces to magazines for several years! I just keep trying, but so far, nothing…"

Amelia couldn't believe it. His work was magazine quality in her opinion. She told him so. "Well, I'll just keep trying. Can't sell a piece to a magazine if I'm not trying, right?" he reasoned, clinging desperately to a cheerful tone of voice as his expression grew dark.

Amelia nodded and thought how they were alike in that way: tenacious. Their birthdays were very near each other's. *Stubborn Capricorns.* They worked hard and didn't give up. Looking up at his face as she sipped her cocktail, she noticed for the first time that he was very handsome. His modesty blended with his confidence made him appear even more attractive to Amelia, not to mention his classic style. He was also smart and kind, easy to talk with. Someone she could trust being alone in a photography studio with.

Burton had a lot going for him. Amelia wondered how many models had been attracted to him and put the moves on him. He had told her once before about a model soliciting him for money in exchange for sex. Amelia could see how sad it had made him. He was in it for the art, not to mention devoted to his wife. Some Greek goddess, as he often lovingly described her.

Burton would often regale Amelia with stories about his beautiful wife. He would blush and stumble over his words if he wanted Amelia to pose nude. She romanticized the way that he was a gentleman with her, and also his faithfulness to his wife.

After they devoured their tacos, they rushed out of the restaurant so that Burton could shuttle Amelia off to her next shoot. The sky was even darker and the clouds seemed to hang lower now. A murder of crows flew by, causing Amelia to stumble a little on her way to the car as she stared up at them. Crows had always made her nervous but she didn't know why.

They got a little lost and she wound up being a bit late. If the GPS couldn't find a place, Amelia was screwed, even if she had been somewhere before; since she was not a driver, she didn't always pay close attention to streets or landmarks when she was riding somewhere. Ordinarily she would have been filled with dread arriving late for a shoot. But she had always been punctual with Hector before this, and she knew that he would forgive her, so she wasn't worried.

They flew past army-green tree after tree until they descended upon Hector's parking lot. Burton got out of his car, always the gentleman, opened her door and then popped the trunk. He extricated her suitcase and pulled the handle up for her, before coming in for a friendly hug. "As always, it's been a pleasure," he told her.

"All mine," Amelia responded, then added, "See you soon!"

"Sure will," Burton said, but his voice was soft. Amelia turned around to see his face smiling, all but his eyes, which seemed to be filled with the same pendulous clouds that hung in the sky.

The clock in Hector's living room always read 3:13. Amelia often found herself compulsively checking the time when she sensed that she might be midway through a shoot with him, and had to remind herself that it wasn't really 3:13. Similarly, Amelia was not really in a photography studio, just the parts of Hector's home that had been converted into shooting spaces: his living room and his den. Hector was a bachelor, although he did have a lady friend, Barbara, who was remarkably average-looking. But Hector made Barbara look like a supermodel when he stood next to her.

Hector was average height, average weight, but with the obligatory middle-aged male gut. He wore glasses that looked like they came from the seventies, and he liked to talk about the days of camera film, as if Amelia couldn't remember. "No, you don't understand: we're talking about the eighties! You weren't even born yet!" he went on. Amelia didn't bother to remind him that she had been born in the eighties. The photographers always thought she was so much younger than they were, and Amelia did not mind that at all.

With his swarthy skin, sunken eyes, and greasy black hair, Hector looked like Gomez Addams on heroin. He didn't have any of the telltale signs of a user, though: his pupils were never pinpoint and his skin was only a normal amount of oily. He never had the ropey saliva strands marrying his upper lip to his lower lip, as Amelia had seen when she worked with opiate addicts. One quality that had always stood out to Amelia, but not to her former colleagues in the treatment center, was a sickeningly sweet smell, like manufactured gardenias, emanating from the pores of all the heroin addicts. But Hector never smelled sweet; he always reeked of old body odor.

Amelia suspected that clinical depression was to blame for his poor hygiene and his hoarding problem. His apartment was littered with garbage and knickknacks. She had seen nothing but empty food and drink containers littering his kitchen counter, wine and liquor bottles surrounding them like a glass fortress. Piles of laundry sat on the couch in the living room and were spread all over the floor, mingling with clothing and sheets that looked unclean. The living room was always inexplicably untidy on shoot days, whereas the den was nearly clean, and they usually shot in both rooms.

Hector's bathrooms were always repugnant. Amelia would inevitably use one of them as a dressing room, and sometimes Hector would use the other to shoot Amelia for bathtub scenes. His bedroom was cluttered with more clean and dirty laundry as well as empty boxes that once held soda cans. His bedsheets had the kind of dirt and hair that don't come from owning a pet; it only comes from eons of not bathing, not changing the sheets, and lying around all day, on days off.

Amelia had only been in his office once, and had noticed immediately that there were empty soda bottles and receipts scattered around the desk, the floor, and the guest bed. There were old jackets and plastic bags hanging out in the bed as well. There was no chair for Amelia to sit on when she needed to sit at his desk to look through his files so that she could pick out some photos for her portfolio. She pushed aside a pile of coats and bags and sat on the edge of the bed. Hector looked at some shots with her, and in his excitement, forgot that his keys were still in his pocket, so when he put his hand down his pants, it was clear to both of them from the jingling sound just how much Hector liked the pictures.

Despite all of this, Amelia had a soft spot for Hector nowadays. She had been working with him for about two and a half years. When Amelia had first met Emma, who was ten years younger than she, it had been at Hector's house in Redmond, Washington, just outside of Seattle. Emma lived in Portland and had been excited to discover that Amelia did, too. They both traveled constantly for work because they had already shot with all the amateur photographers in Portland, and they also both had regulars in many other cities. For someone less inhibited in her photos and videos than Amelia was, Emma was weirdly shy in her personal life and told Amelia that she only had one other friend. Her other friend, Nancy, was also a model, who went by Isis. "She named herself after the goddess," Emma explained to Amelia, "and she had already built a name and a career for herself when the whole terrorism thing started."

Emma had tattoos all over her body and a level of street smarts that Amelia could never even hope to cultivate. Emma's tattoos were beautiful as they wove a story around her voluptuous body. She wasn't thick, but she had about twenty pounds on Amelia, who looked puny standing next to Emma, who was Botticelli's Venus come to life. Emma had the body of a goddess, not Isis. Amelia had heard that Isis had an incurable venereal disease but was still spreading herself all over town as rampantly as a forest fire spreads. But Amelia had also heard, not only from Emma but from the photographers they worked with, that Isis frequently canceled shoots, citing a mysterious illness. Isis was short, youthful in appearance, thick around the middle, pleasantly plump in the tits and ass department, but with skinny legs and arms. She wasn't really young; she was Amelia's age. Somewhere in her mid-thirties, when the exact number doesn't really matter so much anymore. All that really mattered was that you're still in the middle.

Because what could be scarier for a model than going over the hill?

Amelia saw potential for her career to continue every day when she woke up and examined herself in the bathroom mirror. But she didn't take it for granted. She studied her reflection every day, and saw the possibilities, and knew that her age could catch up to her the very next day, and just like that, she could be out of a job. Or only shooting really gross stuff.

They never had to do anything degrading at Hector's place: Amelia and Emma only had to kiss. They could be in their lingerie sometimes. Other times they would be wearing cute dresses, or they would be naked.

Once their arms and legs were entwined as they kissed each other's lips, you couldn't see much of their breasts or genitals; *implied nudity*, they called it. Though they were always actually nude, rather than just suggesting that they were.

When Amelia had answered Hector's ad, she had understood he was gathering material for a coffee table book he was working on. It would come out as soon as he had enough shots of different models, and he had told her he already had a publisher interested. So after he shot Amelia kissing Emma, Amelia returned to Redmond to lock lips with Amethyst, Monique, and—Amelia's favorite of the other women—Natalia. After two years of kissing different models, and then eventually just kissing Natalia many times over, Amelia came to understand that there was no book. This was a private collection kind of situation.

Not that Amelia minded working for a private collector. She was just more accustomed to knowing upfront that the photos would never be released to the public. Every time she went over to Hector's house, she got paid one hundred fifty dollars per hour to make out with gorgeous models for a minimum of two hours, an average of three hours. Some of the days that she shot with Natalia, their shoots had been extended for an extra hour or two, all the way up to five hours once. The day that Amelia did nothing but kiss Natalia's lips and neck for five hours straight, occasionally touching the curves of her hips and her slender shoulders, but never groping either of those size C breasts that were the only large things on Natalia's frame, never slipping a finger inside of Natalia's panties as she had longed to—that was probably the longest, most grueling work day of Amelia's professional life. Years later, she would also remember it as hotter than all the times she and Natalia had had full sex.

Natalia was a petite Italian woman, another model nearing middle age who didn't show it, except for maybe a little bit around the eyes. She was loud in a way that you wouldn't expect from a person of such small stature.

She laughed wildly, and her English wasn't great, and the more excited that she became in conversations, the more she would yell, "I know, I know!" in response to her own stories. Natalia was the same dress size as Amelia, but they looked different: Amelia was small but she had more muscle and her skin was a little more supple. Natalia had nothing but skin and bones, except for those perfect, perky 32Cs. Amelia was a 34C, but of course she noticed the way other women's breasts stood up more than she could give her own tits credit for. But Amelia was often complimented for being well-endowed herself. One lover told her that it was unexpected: she didn't flaunt her gifts or embellish them with a pushup bra. She just wore her dresses, and when they came off, partners noticed that she wasn't small all over, as she appeared when she was clothed.

Amelia had tried to date both Emma and Natalia, although she had known going into these relationships that both women had boyfriends. With Emma, Amelia had had to break it off before she got too attached and became frustrated that she couldn't have more. With Natalia, Amelia felt concerned that Natalia couldn't give all her heart to another woman, even if she wasn't in a relationship with a man.

Natalia confirmed her suspicion as they wrapped up their most recent shoot at Hector's home, although technically they were still lovers, outside of the realm of photography.

"I've been dating," Amelia announced before taking a sip of her malbec. She was sitting across from Natalia later in their favorite pretentious wine bar in Redmond after the shoot.

"Oh, yeah, who you dating?" Natalia asked in her heavy accent.

Amelia explained that she had seen a couple of different women lately, and that, although it had not led anywhere, she was excited about putting herself out there.

"With women?" Natalia cried. "No, you can't be serious!"

Amelia confirmed that she was serious.

"I don't know," Natalia started, lowering her voice suddenly, "don't you feel like, with a woman, it's fun but … there's something missing?"

Amelia laughed and shook her head. "No, it isn't like that for me."

Natalia drove her to the train station after they finished their drinks. "I'm sorry. I don't think there's anything wrong with it," Natalia assured her on the way there. "It is just different for me. I did not really see women in relationships with women in my country, and I think being with women is fun, but I could never be serious." She changed lanes. "But it's great for you!" she added, her eyes darting from the road to Amelia, who smiled only on one side of her mouth. "You must like a lot of American women," Natalia suggested.

"Sometimes. I tend to go for a lot of European women too," Amelia said quietly, her cheeks turning a little pink against her will.

"Aww," Natalia cooed quietly. Then she turned a corner and belted out, "Here we are!"

Amelia and Natalia embraced and said good-bye, and Natalia sped off. The wine had gone to Amelia's head, along with the scent of Natalia and the rush of talking quickly, trying to get a word in edgewise with her chatty friend. She pulled out an American Spirit and took several long drags off it before she entered the train station. She felt light-headed from the cigarette and realized that she hadn't eaten much, so she made her way to the vending machines, and watched an old man struggle to force a dollar bill into one of them with his shaky hand. She felt blue, wishing she'd gone home with Natalia one last time, as she sensed that the sexual part of their relationship was dying. *Why would you miss something you never really had, something that was never real?* she wondered, then shrugged off the question as she stepped onto that familiar train that always took her back to Portland late at night, at the end of another lucrative business trip.

4. October 24

Everything was in slow motion, as if Mia were constantly moving under dark, murky water. She couldn't eat, couldn't feel any hunger—except for the acute longing for Burton to return. *If you don't, I am going to lose this curvy Greek body that you revered,* she told the husband who lived inside her mind. Friends and family members rallied to bring her pasta dishes, casseroles, even some of her Greek favorites like moussaka and spanakopita. Mia kept everything in the freezer.

Feeling weak from crying all night and drinking too much wine, Mia finally ate the night before Burton's funeral. She devoured three baklavas. *What a fine dinner,* her inner critic snarked. That was her own voice, not Burton's. But the gentler side of herself countered, *Well, that will keep you going for a while, at least.*

The next day, the funeral itself was a blur. Her aunt gave her something for anxiety and it compounded the feeling she had of moving underwater, but she was grateful to be able to sit still and not make a scene. She and

Burton had both always been so poised when they were out together. She felt that she would have made him proud, crying silently, not moving from her pew.

Mia took a limo to her home, where the wake would take place. Everything sped up a bit when she greeted visitor after visitor. Everyone hugged her, crying hard, or looking uncomfortable, not knowing what to say. Or imploring her to eat. Her cousin Alexis asked her what she needed, if there was anything she could do for Mia. That was the greatest kindness she had found: someone offering to do anything she needed, rather than imposing their own ideas of what might help.

The Xanax must have been wearing off. Mia felt overheated and nauseated all of a sudden. She ran to the bathroom and splashed cold water on her face. After she patted her face dry, she stared at it in the mirror. *Thirteen years with you, and it's now just me,* she thought. *Me without you.* She struggled to recognize herself.

When she returned to the living room, she tuned out what everyone was saying around her. She was glad to be standing alone then, fading into the background, as everyone was engaged in conversation with each other. People chatted but in hushed voices, out of respect, and it all melted into a discordant, bass murmur, something like a church hymn. She took advantage of her sudden invisibility and retreated to her bedroom. Mia was suddenly bone-tired, and she lay down on her bed.

When she awoke, Mia felt sticky, a cool sweat soaking her skin and even a little bit of the sheet and pillow beneath her. She sat straight up, feeling panicked at first, until she realized that she must have dreamed that Burton had died. *I have to tell you about this crazy dream I had!* she thought she would tell him. She felt intoxicated by how calm and relieved she felt, with every muscle in her body beginning to relax.

The cloud she was on dissipated abruptly when Mia heard low voices still blending together in the living room. The rest of the day came back to her and she realized she must not have been asleep for very long, if the wake persisted on the other side of her bedroom door. She would have to make her apologies later; Mia wasn't coming back out.

She dug around in the medicine cabinet in the master bathroom, hoping to find another pill she could take. Perhaps Burton had left an antianxiety or pain med behind after some dental visit. *You spent so much time going to those dentist appointments that I set up for you, to avoid losing that beautiful smile, or incurring an infection that could go straight to your heart, and for what?*

Unable to find anything, Mia returned to their bedroom. She wondered if Burton might have hidden anything in his underwear drawer. She shook her head, tried to brush off the implausible idea. If she had drugs, she might hide them in her underwear drawer, so that no one would find them in the medicine cabinet. But that doesn't mean that Burton had comported himself in the same manner. Plus, she had never looked through Burton's drawer and or gotten into any of his other private things. She worried that it would be disrespectful, even now.

Mia sat down on the bed for a moment, on her hands, and rocked back and forth. She tried to rid herself of the urge to violate Burton's privacy. To her disappointment, she found that it lingered. After rushing back to the dresser, she didn't hesitate a moment longer: she yanked open the drawer and saw all her husband's boxer-briefs neatly folded and peacefully co-existing with all the balled-up pairs of socks that she had lovingly purchased for him throughout the years. Burton hadn't been careful to remember to buy practical items for himself after his socks and underwear had begun to wear out. He had been so fond of luxury that he only remembered to get himself the things that he wanted, not the ones that he truly needed.

She knew it wouldn't matter if she rumpled his underwear, but still she took care to lift each article gently and not disrupt the order in Burton's drawer. She heard no pill bottles rattling around, but her fingers felt something glossy and thin. Delicately, she removed it and brought it up close to her face as her whole body trembled. She struggled to get her eyes to focus so she held the object up so that it was eye level.

A woman with long, pale blue hair smiled back at her from inside a photograph, her expression enticing. She had tiny brown freckles on her nose, and milky white skin, and with her almond-shaped eyes, she reminded Mia of a cat. Her back was arched so that her ample, naked bosom stuck out like a shelf. By contrast, the woman's waist was microscopic.

Mia had an hourglass figure, or so she had been told. *But you'll never achieve a waistline like that*, the inner critic whispered. And the softer version of Mia immediately warned, *perhaps if you don't start eating, you will.*

Still scanning the Polaroid, Mia saw that the subject's bare legs were long and lean. One knee was crossed over the other, and her hands rested on them, while her shoulders were slightly shrugged in a playful pose. Her red lips were parted wide, as if in surprise, but the corners of her mouth were curling upward to show that she was joyful. She expressed a simple form of femininity: she looked like the type of woman who wanted to please a man above all else, and would forgive him for anything.

Mia wondered if she could forgive Burton of any trespass. He had been a good husband. She had always trusted that he had been faithful. Now she didn't know what to think. *Had this woman been his lover?*

She didn't want to think that, but she felt herself losing touch with reality. Everything she knew swirled around her as she struggled to pluck one facet of her life from the air in an attempt to make any sense of it. *You didn't eat at the service*, the ghost-husband gently reminded her in her head. *That probably isn't helping keep you steady.* After that, Mia saw nothing more and fell to their bedroom floor.

5. October 25

Living in Portland, Amelia felt, for the most part, that she could be herself. She was open about her day job as a model, and her close friends were privy to the details of her night job. She proudly identified as a sex worker, and sometimes, playfully, even referred to herself as a hooker, after that first night in Reno. There was no shame or self-deprecation in her voice when she said this. She wouldn't tone it down: she preferred to be blunt and honest. Perhaps she also enjoyed the shock value a bit. At times she supplied services that didn't feel sexual to her at all but were titillating to the other participant, and therefore still fell into the category of sex work, in Amelia's opinion.

Trampling, for example.

Stepping on a man for money was sort of meditative for Amelia. It was grounding for her to dig her toes into the cool skin of his stomach, to feel the squish of his bit of belly fat beneath her heels. Mostly working barefoot or in nylons, Amelia found it less intimidating that way. Her photographer didn't mind. He set up a video camera to roll and then he lay down to become her "human carpet," as he called himself. She was encouraged to hop from his stomach to his lap, squashing his groin with her feet.

"Doesn't that hurt?" Amelia asked him, wincing after the first jump.

"No," Dave started slowly. "It's uh… it's in the right condition that it doesn't hurt the way it would if it were softer."

Amelia nodded to signal that she understood. She was also encouraged to touch her foot to his mouth, stick her toes inside his mouth. Foot worship, she was told, was the name for what he did to her toes. Sometimes he kissed them bare and other times she wore little slip-on nylons, just barely covering her feet, or tights or stockings.

"It's easy stepping on a guy for money," she told a small group of new friends that she made at a bar one night. Amelia didn't talk about her fetish modeling often with strangers. But later, after she had finished stepping on Dave, she'd gone out to a tavern in Old Town, and with a few drinks in her, she told her new friends about her job.

A handsome Canadian man, sipping some pink, girly drink (for which he'd caught hell from his friends), asked, "How did you find yourself in this business?"

Amelia took a drink of her whiskey on the rocks, shook her head, and sighed. "I don't really know. I've always wanted to create art, or at least be involved in the process. I had to settle for being a muse: I failed at painting, drawing, creative writing… For a while I wanted to be a singer-songwriter, but I don't know how to play any instruments. And I've never been able to write a song that I liked."

"Here's how you do it!" another man in their group cried out, and then crooned, "'It's easy! Stepping on a guy for money!' You'll have a hit song there!" Everyone howled with laughter.

Amelia thought the Canadian gentleman, called Camden, was cute, even though she didn't usually go for blonds. His male traveling companion, Gael from Mexico, had dark, curly hair and was more Amelia's speed, when she was in the mood for a man. *The improv songwriter.* His arm was proprietarily draped around a lady friend. His girlfriend was beautiful: long-necked like a swan. *Or a model.* She sat with perfect posture, to look slimmer, or perhaps to discourage her boyfriend from continuing to throw his arm around her shoulders. Amelia was enjoying the whole exchange: she was more accustomed to being the traveler and meeting locals. She wanted to know more about them, how the three of them wound up traveling to Portland together, but the group was still focused on Amelia.

Chugging his bottle of beer, wearing a proud smile, Gael goaded Amelia further to document all her unusual jobs in fetish photography and sex work. Playing nonchalant by shrugging and then changing the subject, Amelia knew it would nag at her later: she *should* document those stories in some way. She had had the impetus in the past but had never pursued it, had never made any time for exploring the urge.

The way that her desire wound up manifesting itself was unexpected for Amelia. She didn't chronicle the meetings with photographers by writing about them in her diary, or trying her hand at songwriting again. Instead she bought a digital camera on sale at a department store. *How could she pull this off?* she wondered. She wanted to know about *them.*

Dave, the trampling guy, was an easy mark. A lot of the photographers mainly wanted some younger woman to talk to and spend time around. They gave away the helpful details in their dialogues with Amelia at photo shoots: where they worked, if they had "day jobs"; where their wives worked; where they went to the gym; what they did for fun; whether they had dogs or kids they might take to the park. It was all there. Amelia squirreled away these facts as they fell from photographers' lips, stowed them in her back pocket.

Dave was younger than the average man whom Amelia worked for: he was probably in his late thirties. He was almost handsome, more so than the prototypical amateur photographer, but he had a nervous laugh and a propensity to blush that made him less imposing as a man. Amelia liked that because she felt safe with him. He was unmarried, he said, and worked in retail. Emma had introduced them. "I think he still lives with his parents," she had told Amelia over brunch one day. "*And he works in a shoe store.*"

That didn't surprise Amelia, but she wondered how he came up with the dough to pay his models. She took fifty dollars an hour from him, which was the lowest amount that she would accept for clothed fetish work. He explained it all at their next shoot, how he sold the videos to viewers online, usually only selling a few clips a month, making back just enough money to pay for his next shoot. He had many fans of his previews and photos, and hoped that more fans would start becoming patrons of his art.

As he spoke more about his life, Amelia dug her toes into his rib cage, and her mind wandered to how she would execute her plan. She casually glanced at an alarm clock, facing them on a dresser, as they shot in her studio apartment. Much to her surprise, she saw that their time was up. *Not 3:13 here*, she had thought to herself in the middle of it. Sometimes the hour passed so slowly, and sometimes it passed as swiftly as an arrow shot from an archery bow. She made one final jump from his chest to his groin, and then hopped off him.

Dave had often mentioned the part of town where he lived—not far from Amelia's studio—and what park he would walk his dog in. Amelia had to be stealthy. She couldn't show up in the park dressed as herself, of course. Her pale blue hair, you could spot a mile away. She couldn't rely on sunglasses and a trench coat: those were the accessories of models, not spies. The best items she could come up with were baggy jeans, a sweater, a beanie covering her hair. Sunglasses would have to be donned, but nothing glamorous. She wore the kind of shades a dad would wear for an outing by the water, something procured at a gas station.

Amelia waited at Unthank Park all day one Wednesday. She knew that Dave's days off from the shoe store were Wednesday and Saturday, but fewer people would be out on a Wednesday. After waiting for hours, Amelia saw Dave and his cocker spaniel come out of a nearby town house. An elderly woman opened the door after Dave had just closed it behind him. "Wait a sec, he changed his mind," she announced. "He wants to come with you."

A little boy ran down the front stairs and followed Dave and the dog into the park. Amelia's big eyes grew even wider in disbelief. *That's why he lives with his parents!* Amelia thought. *He's probably a single dad!* She had not expected him to be a parent.

Watching them play, she raised her camera with trepidation. *Careful,* she instructed herself. Amelia didn't want to photograph the child. It seemed worse, somehow, photographing a child against his will versus a grown-up. But Amelia didn't want to exploit anyone: she wanted the photographs only for herself. A private collection of her own was a thrilling concept.

The little boy pulled a sling out of his pocket and was shooting rocks into bushes. He was careful not to aim it toward other children, adults, or dogs. *I bet he likes archery too*, Amelia thought. She had made slings and arrows and archery bows out of twigs and sticks and rubber bands when she had been a girl. A painful memory came back to her of losing her archery bow and crying, her parents laughing nervously at how important it was to her. "So you're really into that…*archery*, huh?" her mother asked, eyeing her father and not her. Amelia couldn't forget. She had been a girl with short hair, running around with no shirt on, having crushes on her girl friends. It was at that age when Amelia thought perhaps there had been some mistake and she was meant to be a boy. Maybe the mysterious little nub between her legs would grow longer, like something the boys had. She was six years old at the time. Her parents eyeing each other with concern over her predilection toward archery reaffirmed her belief that she wasn't getting the whole femininity thing down.

There she was now, standing in Unthank Park, a tall, slender woman. When she would go home later and remove her shapeless jeans and the rest of her disguise, she would be nothing but pure femininity, standing naked before the tub.

Amelia finally focused her camera on Dave. He stood with his hands jammed into his pockets, watching his dog and the young boy run off to play, a look of desperation or anxiety, or maybe hope, in his eyes.

After she got her shot, Amelia returned home to the small apartment where she barely ever stayed anymore. Finding herself on the road more often than not, she had hardly decorated and had minimal furniture. She liked having room to dance at home more than she liked owning possessions anyway. "This place looks like Holly Golightly's apartment," her friend Noah had teased her once. Amelia did make an effort to keep her bathroom clean and inviting though, even if it was sparsely decorated, as baths were one of her favorite indulgences.

Twirling her long hair until it made a small bun, she secured it in place so that her blue hair dye wouldn't run out into the bath water. She sank down into the tub. It was nearly dark in her small bathroom except for the light of a few candles. The hot bath caused steam to rise off Amelia's smooth skin, and she inhaled it deeply, trying to plot out whom she would shoot next.

6. November 1

Mia scoured the depths of Burton's desk drawer in his home office, desperate for more evidence that could point to an indiscretion. She didn't want him to be a cheater, but she wanted to stop feeling crazy, even if it meant having her worst fears confirmed. And yet a voice inside her reminded her that she did not really want that. There was a sleek, clean version of Burton still following her around, his image not yet sullied, only suspect. Mia yanked out another drawer, turned it over, and, after not having found anything helpful, she screamed. The hot tears that she had grown accustomed to falling from her eyes began to escape and hit her cheeks again. She took a break and headed to the kitchen.

It had only been a week since Burton's funeral, but everything was constantly changing: Mia no longer starved herself; she shoved everything she could find into her mouth, stuffed it down to fill the vacuous void inside of her. She sat down on the tile floor after grabbing a bag of Cheetos and a bottle of a petite syrah that she or Burton had procured on one of their trips and had probably been saving for a special occasion. Or else it was their local vendor, a little wine shop in downtown Bothell, just north of Seattle. *Don't remember, don't care,* she thought petulantly, uncorking the bottle. Her inner critic spoke up again: *Cheetos and wine for dinner?*

Shrugging off the derisive voice, Mia stuck a fistful of Cheetos into her mouth and chewed. She washed them down with the warm wine. It was woody and smooth, not too tart or sweet. It was perfect. *You would have liked it,* she told Burton.

What are you doing? Dear Deceased Husband asked her, staring at her sitting on the floor with a mixture of judgment and pity in his eyes. *You're better than this. Why do you want to tear us apart?*

Mia sneered at him inside her mind. *Why weren't* you *better, huh?* she asked him. Imagining him holding the blue-haired woman from the photograph, his arms around her and his thoughts on her and not on Mia, she shivered, and then took a big swallow of wine to wash the image away.

After grabbing a spoon out of the kitchen drawer, she pushed around the frozen items in the fridge until she unearthed a pint of vanilla ice cream. She would've turned up her nose at Burton's bland choice before all of this. Now she ate indiscriminately. She sat on the floor again with her legs spread and she ate and ate until her stomach burned. *What am I going to do?* she asked herself.

Slowly she drifted back into Burton's study. She thought it looked so vast and empty without him sitting inside, stroking the keys and the mouse of his laptop, engineering some kind of photoshop magic that she couldn't understand. *That is the trick,* her dark side whispered. *You need to get inside of his computer.*

Mia sat down at Burton's desk, feeling like a child playing at her mother's vanity again. After she had pulled out all her mother's different brushes and eyeshadow palettes and lipsticks, she had rubbed everything around on her face, willy-nilly. *Making a mess again.*

Just like you make a mess of everything.

Mia couldn't tell if that was her inner critic or her mother's judgmental voice. Her mother hadn't reproached her all that often, but when she had, it had been bad enough to sting for a lifetime.

She ran both of her hands down her face, trying to get herself to focus. Her fingers were cold and the effect jarred her back into the present. Burton's computer was locked and she didn't expect that it would be easy to break in. After she lifted the top up, the screen lit up and beckoned for her to enter a password.

Every possible option that flew through her mind seemed too trite. Names, and dates, and places that had all meant something to them, maybe? All the choices seemed too obvious for bright Burton. He seemed to creep up behind her just then. She shuddered, looked behind her, and rolled her eyes. Ghost-Burton whispered into her ear then: *think wines.*

Yes, I know you loved your wine. She accepted that his appetite for *vino* could have informed his password choice. *Never mind our anniversary. My maiden last name*, she thought bitterly for a moment, and then pulled herself out of her dark reverie to refocus on the task at hand.

She positioned her fingers over the keyboard and inhaled a deep, sharp breath. *Could it be that simple?* If it was a kind of wine, it would have been his favorite, either his most preferred variety when he purchased the laptop, or, if he were the type to update his password periodically for increased security, he would've changed it to a more recent wine crush.

Mia knew the answer then: Burton was careful, and his favorite wine did change quite often. She struggled to remember the last bottle he was nursing. More often than not, it was a red. If it was a white, it was dry. They had that in common. She grasped at memories of Burton that were spiraling in her mind, but suddenly she couldn't picture him or his bottles clearly. Every memory was foggy. The last image that jumped into her mind's eye wasn't even of him: she pictured herself sitting with her legs sprawled on the kitchen floor, guzzling petite syrah less than an hour before she had begun this mission.

That was his wine of the moment. That's why it was right there in the wine rack in the kitchen, the small one that they kept in the closest proximity, not hidden away in the back of the pantry. Suddenly, Mia felt guilty. She had chugged it, and Burton never got one drop, and he never would.

"Petitesyrah," she typed into the password bar and then hit enter. The word vanished but the screen did not unlock. The password bar requested another entry. Mia sighed and ran her fingers through her hair. It was thick and her natural waves were turning into ratty curls. Although she couldn't recall when she had last bathed or brushed her hair, she knew that there were more pressing matters to attend to, and her fingers hovered over the keyboard again.

Pragmatic Burton wouldn't have spelled the word so plainly, Mia knew. He was a tech guy. She knew that he would have been more discreet. "PeTite$yrah," she guessed next.

It failed.

Mia grunted in exasperation. *Don't give up, kid,* Burton implored her. *You're getting so warm.*

"Pet!t3syr@h," she typed next, and then paused and sucked in a breath before hitting enter.

That time she got in! She finally let out her breath and then her upper body collapsed onto the desk with relief. *Settle down there,* the critic warned. *Whatever you'll find in there, you know it won't be good.*

Mia didn't know whether to believe that. She dove in headfirst though, hoping for the best.

After heading straight for his main file folder, Mia found scores of photography folders within, as she had known that she would. *Where to start?* She opened folders with names of cities, with titles like *Cross-Processed,* and skipped the ones called *Architecture* and *Landscapes.*

A folder called *Chloe* jumped out at Mia. The mouse hovered over the folder, her finger hesitating before she clicked to open it. She was saddened but not shocked by what she unearthed. It was a kick to her stomach, but not a surprise. It was more like something draining from within her, the rest of what was left of her heart and soul.

There was a young woman—much younger than Mia—posing provocatively on a bar stool and on a chaise lounge. The photographs showed her in various stages of undress. She was a bit curvier than the previous woman she had found a picture of. *Corn-fed* was the expression that popped in Mia's head as she eyed Chloe, her body soft and her skin smooth-looking. Chloe's hair was silky and straight, dark-honey colored. She had a few tattoos winding around her arms and waist that somehow didn't detract from her innocent look. Her smile was naive and her eyes were compassionate. There was something else behind her expression, though. Mia supposed that the innocence was an air, and that what she could read in Chloe's gaze was a subtle hint of teasing: Chloe enjoyed playing the Girl Next Door, but she was not really that innocent sweetheart she portrayed. She was the Nude Model Next Door, to someone.

Where does she live? Mia wondered, until the bigger questions came. *Who was my husband? How was he with you?*
Did you fuck?

Mia shuddered. She didn't shrug off her questions, as much as they disturbed her.

Somehow, Chloe, I will find out. Somehow I will find you.

7. November 2

"Look neutral."

What the fuck does that mean?

Amelia was posing outdoors in the fall in Portland. Mercifully, it was not raining. It was one of those dry, chilly yet sunny days, where the gold- and rust-colored leaves and the bright blue sky were contributing as much flair to the scene as Amelia and her photographer were. Amelia wore a tight-fitting sweatshirt for a vegan clothing line. Cruelty-free, American-made wear, their clothing sported slogans to push the vegan agenda, which Amelia was fine with. She was getting paid in trade with clothing, and would also receive a free vegan meal at a local restaurant of her choice, right after the shoot.

It was rare for Amelia to do trade work, but she was vegan, after all, and it wasn't a cheap diet, so the meal was essentially money in her pocket. Plus, she didn't have enough fashion or commercial work in her portfolio. Besides, the sweatshirt *was* cute.

"Cheat to the left," the photographer instructed her. Amelia knew that meant that she was to move to the left, but she had no idea why the photographer would call a move a "cheat." She moved an inch to the left, which seemed to please her lady photographer.

Lila Fox stood out in the amateur photographer world for being female. She was petite, slender, with a blonde pixie cut. She looked so elegant and regal, until she started shooting a model, at which point she became manic and twitchy. She barked those obscure directives: "inch it, be slick." At times, her instructions became overwhelming: "point your left toe, pop your right hip, hand a little higher on your hip, shoulders straight… OK, now, stick out your chin just a little. And lower your head."

Amelia groaned inside when she began to feel like she was playing Twister, contorting her body in so many different directions. But then she always shrugged it off, because Lila always made her look her best, so it was worth it.

Lila took Amelia out for the meal that she had been promised. While Amelia chewed on some tofu that was seasoned to taste like chicken, Lila rambled on as she always did, interrupting herself, apologizing fervently, thanking Amelia too frequently for helping her with her projects. To Amelia, Lila exemplified strength, not just in her fashion photography but also in the art projects that she recruited Amelia for sometimes. They were statements about gender and sexuality. Despite being slightly bothered by how cheap Lila was, Amelia loved helping Lila and spending time with her, and she loved shooting fashion and creating real art.

Amelia inevitably would become uneasy at some point after spending several hours with Lila, when her strong persona would inevitably be chipped down by the constant chirping of "I'm sorry" and "thank you, thank you so much." *You don't have to thank me so much, and you don't need to apologize for anything,* Amelia had thought so many times. But she wasn't really sore at Lila: Amelia was disappointed in the society that had done this to her.

Sipping on the glass of chardonnay that she had ordered with her meal, Amelia listened as Lila regaled her with stories about her recent trips abroad to shoot models and promote her art. A waiter came by and offered to refill Amelia's glass, or to pour one for Lila. "No, this tea is perfect!" Lila insisted, drinking a minty concoction and breathing in the steam with a hearty breath. Somehow it annoyed Amelia, even though she didn't usually mind being the only drinker at the table. Something about choosing tea over wine seemed haughty, unless the person ordering was British. Although Amelia had a few British friends and she knew they all preferred beer. Lila went back to talking about Amsterdam. "You would love it there, Margot," Lila told Amelia, calling her by her modeling moniker.

All the women in the business had stage names. Amelia had chosen Margot because one of her favorite bands was an indie-rock group named Margot and the Nuclear So and Sos. May was her pretend last name, because she liked names that were alliterative.

Emma preferred the same, going as Penni Page when she did porn, and Chloe Clover when she did straight modeling. Natalia was the oddball, preferring to refer to herself only as Clementine on her online portfolio, but never actually going by Clementine in print or at any of her shoots. She befriended photographers on her personal Facebook page so they always took to calling her Natalia. It was hard to find a better name than Natalia, though, for an exotic European model, in Amelia's opinion. Or perhaps she was partial to the name, having met Natalia as Natalia, and becoming immediately enamored with her.

Lila had worked with "Chloe" and "Penni," but never Natalia. Amelia had suggested it, but Natalia thought Lila's artistic work was a little too overtly sexual, and the most that Natalia ever did was pinup, or the kissing fetish. Lila's commercial projects didn't pay enough, and she wouldn't pay for Natalia's travel fees.

One aspect of Lila's art that Amelia appreciated was her focus on real women and their desires. If she had someone slender and tall like Amelia posing in one of her pieces about sexuality, then the model could, like Amelia, have crazy hair, and go with or without makeup. But she also shot women of all shapes and sizes and colors, with varying amounts of body hair, bodies covered with tattoos, as well as ones that were smooth, blank canvases like Amelia's skin was. Piercings, mustaches, strap-ons: women dressed as themselves in her photos and did what they wanted.

Amelia listened to more of Lila's stories of traveling to Europe, and wondered how she could justify paying her models less than one hundred dollars per hour for her blatantly sexual art projects. What else was she doing with her money? Amelia wondered. Amelia would have to find out. She shook her head at herself for moaning internally about not getting paid for Lila's "ethical porn" projects (as Lila called them) but was doing commercial work for her now, basically for free. *It's all about the perks today, and exposure,* she reminded herself. She nearly made herself chuckle, thinking the idea sounded funny, a nude model needing more exposure! But it was the aspiring amateur fashion model, the clothed one, inside of her who needed the work for her portfolio.

Toward the end of their lunch, Lila had mentioned needing to get some art supplies. Amelia had worked in Lila's home before, a posh Pearl-district condo that Lila had said she was leasing from the owner. Amelia waited a while, so as to not be right on Lila's heels, but eventually took the streetcar to Blick, the art supply chain store, figuring Lila was a Blick person. Amelia had had to change up her appearance of course, so she removed her new sweatshirt, which was black and had white lettering that announced to the world that she was "Vegan AF."

Amelia pulled out a beanie cap from her large handbag and put it over her hair, which was done up in a small bun that curled down toward the nape of her neck. Also in her handbag was her digital camera. At the restaurant, just after Lila had left, Amelia had changed into her requisite baggy jeans, plus a loose-fitting t-shirt and a long cardigan. A circle scarf hung around her neck, and the combination of clothing made it hard for Amelia to discern what any of her body parts might look like to an outsider; you could only tell that her face was thin.

Waiting, Amelia perched on a seat at a bus shelter across the street from the store, to see if Lila would come out. After several minutes, Lila emerged, carrying a paper bag. She looked both left and right, as if she were trying to remember which way something was. Lila started left, then turned, stumbling a little, and then bounded off in the opposite direction, this time with a slightly more confident gait.

Amelia followed, walking slowly enough to stay behind Lila, but quickly enough to ensure that she didn't lose her. The dry, autumn leaves crackled beneath Lila's feet as she rushed off to her destination, her footsteps falling down hard on the pavement. Her heel would hit a patch of cement every now and then, a rare spot unadorned with bronze and brown leaves. Her heel came down hard like a hammer. Amelia enjoyed the musicality of the heels, the sidewalk, and the leaves.

Then Lila stopped suddenly in front of a townhouse, and Amelia froze. Lila looked up the stairs and then moved her body in the same direction. She knocked on the front door. It was not a heavy rap, nor was it a light, timid tapping; it was a friendly, unobtrusive knock. Amelia's camera was ready in her hands now. She lifted the lens to her face so that she could be ready.

A couple opened the door and greeted Lila warmly. Their smiles betrayed their recent red wine intake as well as their agenda for the rest of the evening. Quickly Amelia snapped a picture of the trio on the porch, before the man and woman pulled Lila inside. Through the front window, Amelia could see that all three of them had moved into the dining room, and the man handed Lila her own glass of red wine. Amelia imagined that the wine they were imbibing was very dry with hints of wood and maybe smoke. The man came up behind Lila, kissing the back of her neck and shoulders, and the woman stood before Lila, and then began kissing Lila's lips. Amelia couldn't imagine what it might feel like. She only knew that it looked like the wings of angels opening to envelop you and welcome you into heaven, to be surrounded by that much love.

8. November 2
(earlier that day)

It didn't take clever Mia long to figure out which key on Burton's ring went into the small lock on his filing cabinet. She yanked it open and pillaged the contents of every folder, but then dropped almost everything she found to the carpeted floor of Burton's office. It felt like hours had passed, during which she found nothing of consequence, but when she sighed and looked over at the clock on the desk, she saw that only several minutes had passed. *Time dilation.*

Mia had taken a Xanax, for anxiety. The numbing effect was almost soothing, but she couldn't hide far enough from reality when she was home, with all the drawers in Burton's office and his wretched computer calling out to her, imploring her to investigate. To violate.

Like you violated my trust? Mia asked the Burton who haunted their condo. He shook his head, slow and sad. *It might not be what you think,* he suggested.

Just then, she discovered the file folder labeled *"Releases"* and pulled out contracts. She eyed each one quickly, seeing words flash as she shuffled the pages: *model, photographer, agreement, compensation, alias, hereafter known as, real name.* Then the moniker *"Chloe Clover"* jumped out at her, followed by her real name, *Emma Davis.*

Next Mia noticed Emma's mailing address, phone number, and email address. *Bingo.*

After weighing her options, Mia decided that email was less intrusive than a phone call. She tugged on her heavy hair and wondered where she should start. Then abruptly the words rushed out of her like water from a busted pipe. She had so many questions! Mia paused, and then erased most of them. It was too much. She needed to ease her way in.

Noticing that Emma's home or mailing address was in Portland, Mia asked if she would be back to the Seattle area any time soon, and if she wouldn't mind meeting up with Mia for coffee. She had some questions about modeling and would love to pick Emma's brain, she wrote. She added that she wouldn't mind compensating Emma for her time.

The aroma of the coffee brewing in the kitchen was enticing Mia, so she hit "send" and left the office. After pouring the coffee into one of Burton's large mugs, adding a little cream and sugar, Mia stirred the contents of the cup and then took a sip, enjoying the warmth that spread throughout her body. It was a chilly morning in Seattle, especially for those who lived right on the water. Mia went into the living room and started a fire in the fireplace.

Mia went back into Burton's office, where she had left her own laptop. She had been spending too much time in that room lately. She brought her computer back to the living room, curled up under a throw on the couch, pulled the laptop open. She was surprised to find a response from Emma in her inbox already.

"Hi, Mia,

I'll be back in Seattle again soon. I can do coffee. What part of town are you in?"

She listed some options for times and dates when she could meet Mia, which were only a couple of weeks away. Emma asked how much she could expect to receive in compensation. Mia wrote back after choosing the soonest availability that Emma had open, and offered her one hundred dollars for an hour of conversation in a cafe in her neighborhood. Mia had no idea what rate would be reasonable, but she didn't want to lowball her. Emma replied swiftly and accepted the offer.

On the morning of the day they had planned to meet, a couple weeks after Mia had sent the email, Mia awoke to the cold again. Now that it was getting later in the autumn, she found that she could at least count on the chilly air to be there to greet her each morning. She started her fire in the fireplace and drank a café au lait in the living room before she left for the cafe, thinking of Burton. In the mornings before work, sipping coffee at their dining table, even though he would invariably go through a drive-through and pick up more on his way to the office, he would always say to Mia, "I need coffee to get to my coffee!"

The cafe she had chosen was just a few blocks from her home. Mia walked briskly, instinctively, not paying attention to the streets that she passed, barely noticing if cars were coming or not when she crossed the street. The air was so frigid and though Mia had dressed for it, it still felt too harsh to her bones, the icy cold that crept into her skin.

When she arrived, she hung her coat on a rack near the front door and then scanned the room. No one there resembled Emma. Mia's body relaxed: she had more time to prepare.

Mia took a seat in the back of the cafe, at a booth by a window. She kept her eyes trained on the parking lot, wondering if Emma would pull up in a car, or ride in on one of those rented bikes or scooters. She decided that the latter would be cooler, and might endear Emma to her.

To her dismay, Emma was driving a basic white car, pristine and most likely a rental. She saw the model get out on the driver's side and recognized her instantly. Emma was beautiful with her golden hair and her skin slightly tanned. With her clothes covering all her tattoos, she exemplified the girl-next-door persona even better than she managed to do in her photographs with just her curves and those impish expressions that she wore on her face. Mia thought then about how much work it might be for a model to come up with different poses, various looks. To be in the spotlight all day and to have to project myriad feelings. *How draining it must be*, she thought.

Emma came in through the back door and surveyed the cafe, stopped looking around when (Mia knew) she spotted the only middle-aged woman in the room and had to assume it was her date. Still she walked up to Mia with a touch of trepidation, paused as she stood before her and then asked, "Are you Mia?"

Mia nodded and then tilted her head to suggest subtly that Emma should sit down. She did so, and then stared at Mia, waiting for her to speak. A long minute passed while Mia considered how to start. Emma's face wasn't sweet while she waited. She looked Mia up and down, as if trying to assess what her motive was for inviting her here. Emma appeared much older now, tough and street smart. Mia matched her gaze as they silently tried to figure each other out.

Finally Emma broke the ice. "Listen," she said in a hushed voice, "if you want anything extra, besides just talking, I can tell you how much I charge for extras."

Trying to fight her skin from reddening, Mia cleared her throat and shook her head. It felt like she was shaking it a little too long, so she forced herself to stop. "No, that's OK," she started, careful not to sound like she judged Emma's assumption. "I really just want to talk with you about your modeling. You see, I found your pictures, and your model release form, in my husband's office. He…" She struggled not to choke on the words, then finally pushed them out. "He passed away recently."

Emma's face softened, and she became the good girl again. "I'm sorry," she said, then rolled her eyes at herself. Mia understood how some people said what they thought they were supposed to say and then cringed when they knew that it wasn't enough. Mia could feel her own expression relax, and she thanked Emma. "Who was he? What was…his name?" Emma asked softly.

"Burton," Mia told her. "Burton Hughes." Every time she spoke her married name, she thought of how much more refined it sounded than her own maiden name, Christopoulos. Her Greek last name sounded wild in comparison, as everything about her family's culture had seemed more exotic to Burton when he had joined her family.

Frowning and shaking her head, as if she were trying to dislodge her memories, Emma said, "I think I only shot with him once. My friend Margot shot with him a bunch more times though. She also comes to Seattle a lot, if you want to talk with her."

"Thank you for telling me," Mia responded. She began to dig around inside of her purse, suddenly flustered. "I should give you this before I forget," she said, and pulled out a crisp hundred dollar bill from her bag. She offered it to Emma by sliding it across the table quickly and keeping it low. Emma snatched it up just as hastily.

Mia took a sip of coffee, and then realized that Emma didn't have anything to drink yet. She couldn't help but blush then. "I'm so sorry!" she exclaimed. "Can I buy you a coffee, or tea, or something?"

Emma stood up. "Nope," she replied with a coy smile. "You overpaid for our meeting. I'll get it." As Emma strolled over to the counter, Mia pulled out her phone and quickly typed a word in her notes app: "Margot."

When Emma returned with her tea, Mia noticed her tame beverage choice, and only then did she take in what Emma was wearing: tight leggings, loose crop top sweater, hip pack instead of a purse—the kind of garments Mia had seen in fashion magazines, in spreads advertising streetwear. She had on sensible but loud, brightly colored sneakers that reminded Mia of the eighties. She had taken off her puffy jacket when she had first arrived, but Mia hadn't noticed right away how dressed down Emma was. She wondered if it was Emma's usual decorum or if she was more relaxed because she was meeting with a woman. But then Mia remembered how Emma had offered other services, and she decided that Emma was probably pretty casual in her dress all the time. She must have known that her young body and her sweet face were enough to close the deal.

"I'm sorry, but can I ask you an awkward question?" said Mia.

Emma had just sat down in their booth again and she put down her cup and responded, "Oh, yeah, I don't mind." She shrugged to emphasize how cavalier she was about her work.

Mia let out a breath unconsciously and then tipped her head back and sucked in a new breath. She wasn't sure if she was ready for the answer or not. She asked the question anyway. "You mentioned that you do 'extras.' And the pictures I saw, they weren't exactly pornographic, but they were… suggestive. Did you and my husband ever…do anything, besides shoot?"

Emma's face, so angelic as she pondered what Mia might have meant for a moment, suddenly broke into a wry smile, and then she was the tough girl again. "Oh, you mean, did we have sex?"

Mia frowned and tried not to shudder, just thinking of it. "Well, yes."

"No," Emma replied, and she kept her eyes locked on Mia's. "He was a real photographer, and a real gentleman too. He just wanted to take some pictures. A lot of guys try other stuff, even if it wasn't negotiated up front, but Burton didn't."

Mia sighed a heavy sigh, and thanked Emma. She felt a cold rush of relief throughout her body. "You said that your friend Margot might be back?"

"Oh definitely," Emma assured her. "She usually comes here, like, once a month."

As Mia was about to leave, gathering her purse, Emma added, "I don't think that Amelia—that's Margot's real name—would mind if I just gave you her email address. That way you don't have to track it down in the releases." That knowing smile came back to her face. Mia thanked her again and told Emma she would really appreciate that. Emma nodded and told her she'd email it to her. Mia waved good-bye and then grabbed her coat from the coatrack and crept back out into the biting cold.

9. November 18

Amelia rode the Caltrain from San Francisco to Palo Alto. She was on her way to shoot "damsel in distress." It had first been described to her as a style of photography that involves a woman being tied up, fully clothed, usually in a business suit or girl-next-door attire. Using model networking websites made it easy to obtain references before working for a photographer, which helped assuage any fleeting fears that crept into Amelia's mind regarding safety and working with new people.

The whole concept of the genre struck Amelia as sort of silly: Why would someone be so turned on by seeing a woman tied up who was not even showing any cleavage? Damsel in distress photo shoots often paid well, even better than some of the offers that Amelia frequently received to model in ropes with no clothes on.

The train slowed to a crawl as it pulled into the idyllic, affluent suburb. The photographer came to collect her at the Palo Alto Caltrain stop. Roger was middle-aged, overweight, mostly bald but sporting a tenuous comb-over.

He was wearing a worn-out t-shirt and baggy jeans held up by a decrepit leather belt. He stepped out of his old truck in sneakers, to help her get her suitcase into the back. Amelia was immediately struck by how his face and all its features seemed larger than average: big eyes with swollen bags beneath them, huge honker of a nose, his lips like two dead trout. Subtly examining the rest of him while he drove, Amelia noticed that Roger's hands were also quite large. *The better to choke you with, my dear.* She shuddered. *None of that,* she thought, scolding her brain.

A gentleman in Portland, whom she had met online, had propositioned her long ago to expand her portfolio to include damsel in distress, and had explained all about what the term meant. He had told her that he preferred to shoot in hotel rooms, and had asked her to meet him at the old Red Lion, which was now a local boutique hotel. Thus he had cemented his identity as Ron Red Lion.

Amelia wouldn't feel nervous working with Ron now, but the jury was still out on Roger. She mentally recorded all the turns he made as he drove them to his place—just in case she needed to know. She had had a good feeling about Roger when they'd talked online, and he hadn't done anything to make her nervous so far. She just ran a little bit overly anxious by nature.

Roger Palo Alto was the name she had given him in her list of phone contacts. They made small talk on the way to his home studio. To Amelia he seemed genial, telling her about his wife, asking Amelia questions about her own life. The adrenaline rush she had gotten from the fear of climbing into a stranger's truck and heading off to his home, knowing she would soon be tied up, was beginning to wear off.

When they arrived at his house, he had her sign a standard model release, signing away her rights to the photographs in exchange for cash. Then Roger looked over Amelia's wardrobe options. He wasn't crazy about the shoes she had brought so he suggested that she wear a pair of his wife's heels. Roger asked her to put on a dress suit and thigh-high stockings, and then he positioned her in the hallway near his front door. He described the scene for her: "You're just getting home from work, and suddenly you discover that someone is waiting for you with ropes and he wants to tie you up."

Amelia acted out the scenario Roger had requested, and after he got those shots, he set down the camera and came closer to her to tie her wrists with rope. The doubt jumped back into Amelia's mind. Sure, she had procured several glowing recommendations from other models who had worked with him in the past, and she had seen their portfolios to make sure that the work they stated they had done with him matched the work in his portfolio. *But what if today is the day*, Amelia wondered, her heart beating faster, *when something inside him snaps and he decides he is tired of playing and wants the real thing?* She took a deep breath and listened to her gut, which informed her that her initial instinct had been right: this man wanted to appear professional; Amelia was safe.

Her brain and her stomach were always at odds, it seemed. But she had grown accustomed to quieting her mind long enough to hear what her gut was feeling. It was like there was a flame somewhere in the center of her body. If she could quiet her mind long enough, she could usually concentrate and suss out whether this flame inside of her was shaking and threatening to go out, or if it was steady. This was her barometer for gauging whether her decision was sound or unhealthy.

Her breath quickened a little when he asked if he could put a blindfold over her eyes. "How about if we do that next time, work up to it?" she offered. He was amenable to the suggestion.

After he snapped his last shot, Roger explained that he had to clean up all the ropes, clothing, shoes, camera, and lighting gear. "My wife gets home at five. She doesn't mind that I do this, but I just don't like leaving the evidence everywhere. I like to clean the place up before she gets home, out of respect."

Amelia helped him tidy up. She wondered if his wife really knew what was going on. After his home was back in order, Roger gave Amelia a ride back to the train stop. He helped her out of the truck and handed her her suitcase, after paying her handsomely.

On the Caltrain back to San Francisco, Amelia marveled at how her vivid imagination and trust issues could still lead her into moments of anxiety over working with new people. She set up most of her gigs through a model-photographer networking website called *Model Mayhem.* Back when she had still been a perpetually exhausted night-shift worker at the treatment center, she had dreamed of a more glamorous life, anything artsy that could take place mainly during daytime hours, really. Her old friend from high school, Adele, was a high-art photographer who had shot some nudes as well as some clothed glamour and fashion shots of Amelia, in order to help each of them build their portfolios. After Amelia had uploaded her images onto her new account, she figured that maybe she could use the website to try to find some photographers to try to sell herself to. However, she had not wound up having to do any selling: she had been pleasantly surprised to discover, the day after she had set up her account, that she had received tons of offers from photographers working in various genres.

After wading through all the initial offers, Amelia had not been dissuaded even though her first offer turned out to be an unorthodox request. The photographer was living in a small town in the south, and had offered to fly her out and pay for her hotel stay if she would pose for him. They had exchanged several emails before he got around to fully delineating what he had expected of Amelia.

In retrospect, she realized her first clue should have been that he continued to ask her to define what she had meant when she said that she would be willing to pose nude for *erotic* photography. The Southern man had eventually gotten around to his point: when Amelia had asked him what kind of projects he had been working on, he had responded: "I am working on an erotic open-leg style book and a fetish book on solo female urination." Amelia had replied that she was a tad too conservative to do either project, but would feel comfortable creating something more artistic with him.

The photographer's next response had been: "I'm sorry to hear that you cannot do either of those projects. Your profile says that you do erotic and fetish work. My concern is that, if I am going to spend that kind of money on airfare and the hotel, I really need to get a few images out of the shoot to be able to use for my books, at least the open-leg erotic one. I have a deadline approaching for the female urination book so I really need some shots for that one. Is there any way you would reconsider, please? Even if we had to fake the urination images…"

Young, green Amelia had been so surprised that anyone would try to persuade her to get nude for them so that they could take pictures of her and digitally add urine streams to the images! She had very strict boundaries about what she would and wouldn't do, and anything involving urine, feces, or vomit—her own or someone else's—was something she had been staunchly opposed to.

Amelia had ignored the rest of the photographer's emails but had taken up some local guys on offers for work that sounded a little more vanilla. For a long time, she did not receive another offer that quite matched the level of kink that first one had, but there were several offers that vied for second place: She had often been invited to be tickled or spanked, and once was persuaded to take off and throw her bra at the camera for a flying bra fetish site. The latter was a kink that she had never heard of before, but she quickly learned that if you can do something, *anything*, then someone will have a fetish for it somewhere. Amelia hadn't seen any harm in tossing her bra toward the camera repeatedly until the videographer had obtained enough footage, so she accepted the position while she had been traveling around the Southwest. But she had turned down a half a dozen more offers for boy-girl, girl-girl, and masturbation scenes.

In the beginning she had stayed relatively pure. Amelia wound up mainly working on artistic or sensual projects, some of them featuring tongue-in-cheek light bondage or pinup themes. She couldn't say that she had never felt compromised in those days, but she had grown adept at standing up for herself. She had gotten paid pretty decently to do light stuff. At that point she had no longer been working full time at the treatment center, but had remained on-call there, picking up two or three shifts a week to make ends meet.

After she had realized just what her boundaries would be for the more pornographic work, and stopped listening to the imaginary scorn of her mother or lovers who hadn't known she was considering it but would have been judgmental, Amelia had quieted her mind long enough to feel that flame that navigated where she really wanted to go. She had longed to be completely free from her day job, and to share with the world her own ideas about real female sexuality. After a few years of modeling part time, she knew that she would not realistically be able to get away with only making art and political pornography. But stepping on people, whipping old men, or getting tied up in her old office clothing was easy and did not feel demeaning to Amelia. In fact, she had grown to enjoy the fact that she was helping people achieve pleasure even if it was through a kink that just seemed harmless and nonsexual to her.

Amelia was almost done with the Bay Area leg of her trip, where she had shot not only the damsel in distress set, but other, more hard-core bondage scenes earlier in the weekend. She had been thankful to have the gig in Palo Alto, in between those harder scenes and her impending sex scene, since she had been able to keep her clothes on the entire time she was shooting in Palo Alto. *The better to hide your battered skin.*

Sitting in the train car, she looked down and admired how the ropes had made such deep indentations on her wrists and arms. It turned her on. Roger's large, puffy face did nothing for her, so she kept his image out of her mind, but, focusing on the marks, and imagining that a lover was responsible for putting them there, set off a small fire inside of Amelia. It felt like red wine going from her throat into her belly.

Roger's bloated face, grotesque and cartoonish, crept into her mind's eye. She couldn't fight its cooling powers, the way it acted as a wet blanket. Her thoughts turned to his (most likely) unsuspecting wife. What was she like? What did she do? What did she know? Amelia would've liked to take the train back to Palo Alto later to find out. But their house was nestled so deeply in the suburbs that it wasn't on a bus line, hence the need she'd had for Roger to pick her up at the train stop earlier.

Shrugging off (as best as she could) the urge to run back and peer into their dining room window, Amelia opened a *Vogue* magazine instead. Unlike her model friends, Amelia didn't devour fashion magazines very often: she only enjoyed a few of them from time to time. She found most of them vapid, and much preferred reading books, but she did indulge in a monthly subscription to *Vogue*. The articles were as resplendent as the fashion spreads, in Amelia's opinion. She knew that most of her friends read it too, but because of her predilection toward classic literature, Amelia classified her *Vogue* addiction as a guilty pleasure.

A woman glared at Amelia from inside an ad. "Conceal, reveal, glow. Because you're worth it," the ad promised. She breezed past the media coercion, those beauty myths, and flipped to a two-page spread about the latest supermodel, who was hailed as "too big for the page." Amelia considered the unfair irony that models had to be smaller than anyone else in order to be "larger than life."

Amelia and Natalia both wore a size two. Lila had modeled as a size zero, or "straight-size" model, as they were often referred to, before she made her foray into directing. Everyone who knew any of them in real life thought they were all so tiny, exclaiming how they must be so cold all the time, must be eating nothing but air!

Emma was a healthy size five, but she and Amelia knew a lot of other pro-amateur models who were eights and tens. A couple of models they knew who wore over a size six were constantly having to defend themselves against the "plus size" label.

Models who wore a four or smaller were considered straight-size. Amelia had grown accustomed to going to fashion and pinup photo shoots and being able to choose from wardrobe items that were all sized between two and eight. She shuddered to think of what it would be like if she were a New York fashion model, struggling to find any sample pieces to put on that weren't a zero or a double zero.

Models were meant to represent people, to be examples of human beings. Why then were they required to be smaller than average? *Smaller than life.*

Amelia's stomach was rumbling on the Caltrain, and she thought about what she might eat later that night. She couldn't decide between going out on the town or ordering some takeout. It had been a busy weekend already, and after eating and sleeping, she would be starting off the next workweek with a trip to Nevada. She decided on *DoorDash* and put on another guilty pleasure—a true crime TV show—to entertain her in her modest motel room. Not knowing where the appeal stemmed from, but not really caring, Amelia watched and listened to the gruesome tales until she fell into an uninterrupted slumber, a box of half-eaten Thai noodles making an oil stain next to her on the comforter.

The next day she caught a train to Reno. There had always been something romantic to Amelia about train rides. The train's very whistle was like a beacon calling her from her home, summoning her back onto the road. She had obtained some coke from her friend Genevieve, who lived near Golden Gate Park, just in time for another meeting with Sam.

November 19

All the way to Reno, you've written your own directions, and whistled the rules of change.

Who sang that? Amelia struggled to recall. *Was it R.E.M?* She decided that it probably was, and rolled over to taste her pillow without meaning to. It was then that she noticed she could only breathe out of her left nostril. The right nostril didn't just feel clogged: it felt like it was stuck together with some sort of crust. She wasn't sure if it was mucus or blood, and then she wondered how she had gotten herself into a situation in which she would have to speculate about what was stuck all over the right side of her nose. She got up to face her reflection in the mirror hanging on the wall, next to the TV. *Huh… blood* and *mucus.*

In the throes of a foggy cocaine hangover, she got back into her hotel bed, which thankfully contained no goose down this time. She always called ahead nowadays, or else she had the photographers call ahead, to request a room that was "feather free."

Amelia had one more shoot scheduled later that morning, so she knew that she had to move quickly in order to bathe herself and straighten up the room. She hadn't told Sam that she would be using the room to shoot with another photographer. But Sam was gone; he had driven back to Tahoe. He would never know.

The man she was meeting next was Diego. The last time they had worked together, he had hired her in order to shoot close-ups of her vagina in black and white, an artistic portrait study of sorts, he had explained at the time. Amelia had joked to herself, *Of course: if it's in black and white, it has to be artistic, right?* But actually she loved how all vulvas look different from one another; each was florid in its own unique way, and could be presented as art—provided that the photographer had the right eye.

When she had worked with Diego last, she had been surprised when he had opened the door and stood before her, attractive, aging well, Latin.

She had always had a predilection toward Latin men. Amelia had moved nervously about his studio that day, sometimes babbling, sometimes shy. The way he looked at her, studying her with his dark eyes, made her feel secure that her feelings were reciprocated. When he had asked her if she wanted to help with another series, about the female orgasm, she had not been surprised, nor had she been offended by the suggestion, even though she had only shot boy-girl scenes with a boyfriend first, and then with Sam.

Amelia had shot a multitude of girl-girl scenes. She found that working with another woman lent more verisimilitude to her role in the scene: sleeping with a hot woman was something she did not only for money but for real pleasure. How could she feel as proud if she were to sleep with a middle-age man with a flaccid belly and an average-size (or smaller) penis? This was not the world of professional porn, where perhaps if she were a young model, she could choose any handsome male actor with a large member to be her scene partner. So in feeling compelled to sleep with Diego, so much so that she would have probably slept with him for free if they met in some bar, she found an opportunity to create a piece that was authentic.

Though it hurt her pounding head to do so, Amelia slid out of her messy hotel bed and rushed into the bathroom for her shower. The steam helped to rejuvenate her a little. She had set up some coffee to brew before climbing in the shower, and then could smell it as she inhaled the steam of the shower. The combination was working; she was beginning to wake up. She checked to see if she had stubble on her legs or bikini area. Armpits? No. She was good.

After she had dried herself with the plush hotel towel, cloaking herself in the comfy robe hanging in the bathroom, she sipped coffee. The caffeine kicked in quickly and made it easier for her to brush her long, tangled hair. She often changed the color, but had recently achieved just the right shade of baby blue that she had dreamed of attaining for years. So pale blue would stay for a bit. Maybe she would do something else. Perhaps she would get a pixie cut, she thought, smiling when she imagined how the short blue locks would frame her face.

Applying her makeup in the bathroom mirror, Amelia tried to recall her dreams from the previous evening. Nothing came to mind. Every time she fell asleep on a comedown from coke, she slept fitfully and would never recall any dreams the next day. She realized she was nervous about the impending shoot with Diego. That one time she had done boy-girl with her ex-boyfriend, Noah, they had only planned to pose together for some implied nude, artsy shots, but the heat between them kept building and became overwhelming. They were grabbing each other's hips, holding their mouths in front of one another's to imply that they were about to kiss, until they could no longer contain themselves and they went in for a real kiss, which led them to grab each other harder.

Noah was still a good friend, but they had broken up too many times. They lived on different coasts. They had been having a long-distance relationship, but each of them had been too stubborn to move, so they gave up. They still texted and they looked at each other's pictures of vacations and concerts they attended, separately now, on Instagram. Amelia knew that if she were in the same town as him again, for a visit, she would still feel compelled to sleep with him, even if her brain knew better. It was like he had a piece of her heart and always would, and the flame she carried for him was an ember that could reignite if she had to see his face and be near his body again. She still liked looking at the photos they had made together from time to time, enjoying the juxtaposition of her pale skin pressed against his black skin.

After the fire, she kept an ember / tucked away for a dark December. That was the only poem Amelia had ever written. Structurally, it didn't work as a haiku: it had one syllable too many. But Amelia still liked it. She had carried it around in some small drawer inside of her always, since right after high school, the same way she did with the little ember that she carried for Noah.

Some time after that shoot with Noah, she was offered the gig with Sam. She had slept with Sam twice. She still had some coke leftover from the previous night, and although she was nervous about her impending shoot with Diego, she knew she wouldn't have to coax her body with drugs to accept him. She recalled his face, his dark eyes, his strong-looking body, from when they had last met, and she was already beginning to get wet. So she went without the drugs. She knew that her brain, and her nose, would thank her later for staying sober.

When he arrived, Diego had a large camera bag slung over his left arm. He wore a tight, charcoal gray t-shirt and a pair of jeans that looked new and pristine, and fit snug. He explained his end goal for the project: to show a woman having a real orgasm. In his thick accent, he went on to explain that she could move him anyway that she needed, give him verbal cues, and bring her own fingers or toys into it if she wanted to. "Anything that will make your orgasm authentic," he added. This reminded Amelia so much of Lila's work; her artistic projects were quite similar.

Perhaps Amelia could introduce the two of them one day, she thought.

Although she didn't want to objectify her friend, Amelia let herself entertain the idea of a threesome with Lila and Diego. The photographers were both physically attractive. Lila seemed to Amelia a kindred free spirit, though Amelia was just behind Lila in terms of experience in the industry. Not to mention experience with threesomes. Of course, Amelia didn't know what Diego's proclivities might be. She only knew he was a seasoned artist, originally from Mexico City.

Amelia hadn't found herself attracted to Lila until that night when she had followed her. Whereas Amelia had found Lila's energy sort of chaotic sometimes before, now when she thought of Lila flitting around during one of her shoots, she realized that what had annoyed her before had not been Lila's energy at all: she was like a butterfly that would fly up close to you and flap her beautiful wings around in your face and then, once you reached out to touch her, she flew off again. Lila's energy had bothered Amelia because she couldn't catch it and hold on to it and examine it. She couldn't drink it in or inhale it. She caught a waft of Lila's scent sometimes though. Standing behind her at times while she set up the lights and rearranged pillows and sheets, Amelia had had a good view of Lila's little, toned ass, and she could smell something dark and intoxicating, a perfume that reminded her of a black orchid.

Thinking of Lila's scent in the hotel room with Diego helped calm Amelia for the sex scene, even as it excited her. There was something familiar she seemed to be able to harness and draw into their scene: Lila's bewitching smell. She looked up as Diego continued to adjust the lights, her eyes trained on his full lips.

Usually photographers who were going to act in their own scenes did not kiss their models, even during sex, as it was a tacit agreement in the industry: no kissing on the lips. Amelia had known that going in, mainly from hanging out with Emma. Amelia would bend the rules for Diego. He had bee-stung lips that she wanted to feel on every inch of her body, including her mouth. She hoped that he would go in for the kiss, that she wouldn't have to tell him it was all right. She didn't want to scare him with her willingness to eschew the standard boundary, didn't want to appear too eager, unprofessional.

Diego asked her to lie down on her hotel bed, and he positioned all his cameras in different corners of the room, with a boom mic and one camera just above her. Her breath was caught in her throat. Diego began by running his hands over her naked body, lightly and slowly. He caressed her legs, thighs, stomach, breasts, ran a finger along her collarbone, and then drew a line down her sternum. He stopped for a moment when he reached her stomach, and then brushed her abdomen with his fingers, so softly that she had to stifle a whimper: she was painfully ticklish on her abdomen.

Tracing her hip bones was a better experience. When his fingers got close to her groin, she felt high with excitement. But he stopped touching her abruptly and backed away. Amelia held her breath. Diego leaned forward and began to lick her pussy. She closed her eyes, focused on the feeling of his wet tongue. As her breath and heart rate quickened, she began to move her hips, thrusting to match the movements of his tongue, making sure that she caught every lick. Then she had to grab his head, pull his hair a little to make sure that he remained in the right spot. Her mind grew quiet as her animal instinct took over. She didn't care if she was pulling his hair or grabbing him too hard; she desperately needed to come.

Finally she came, making the loud, guttural sounds that she was familiar with, even as they still frightened her a little; when she came that hard, she felt as if she were coming like a man. She pictured herself as that scared child exploring herself in the bathtub again, not knowing what gender she was meant to be, who she would become.

Diego turned off the cameras and shyly perched himself on the edge of the bed. Amelia felt so delicate and raw as she lay breathless and flushed. Diego had taken off his pants before they had gotten started, and now he stood up to look for them on the floor. Grabbing them by the belt, he started toward the bathroom. Amelia realized that the filming was over already. She hadn't gotten to taste his lips yet. She was so hungry for more. Her phone sat beside her on the bedside table. She picked it up gingerly. Diego was bending over toward the shower, his back to her in the bathroom with the door ajar, putting his pants back on. Amelia caught all of this with a surreptitious picture on her phone.

After breaking down all of his lighting equipment, Diego placed a few hundred dollar bills on the table beside her, next to her phone. Amelia thanked him, and he insisted that the pleasure was all his. She was watching his lips like she was a feral animal and his lips were dinner. *Give them to me...*

"Let me know," Diego suggested, "when you are coming to town again." Amelia nodded and said that she would, silently vowing to return sooner rather than later.

Sadly, Diego never returned her texts or emails when she was planning her next trip to the area. Some people in the industry just turned into ghosts that way, and Amelia had grown accustomed to it, even if it did disappoint her a little in this case. But she did wind up getting that pixie cut she had fantasized about.

10. November 27

When Mia had gone through the thousands of files in Burton's computer, looking at pictures of Amelia, and Emma, plus scores of other models, she had felt unexpectedly aroused in between moments of anger and grief.

Who are you? Who were you? she continued to ask ghost Burton, until she began to wonder about the models, too.

Who are you? What do you feel like? She thought about what she might like to do to them. *Where to start?*

Mia had felt attracted to women before, but Burton had really been her sexual orientation, and her romantic preference for so much of her life. She hadn't anticipated having an identity crisis in midlife. As much as it surprised her, she welcomed the distraction from her sadness. She had come to feel so numb all the time, weighed down by the heavy ache in her heart like an anvil on her chest.

When she fantasized about being with a woman, the warmth seemed to return to her body. She relished the feeling of her heart racing, the blood flowing through her, whenever she touched herself. Sometimes she didn't come out of her bedroom for days, stuck in this in-between world: vacillating between crying and touching herself. *At least you've moved past the wine, Cheetos, and Xanax phase*, she said to herself with a wry smile.

Mia sat up in bed, remembering that she had the email address Emma had given her for Margot, or Amelia, whoever she was. *That beautiful blue-haired kitten*, Mia remembered. She felt woozy from sitting up too fast, after having just made herself orgasm, and then she remembered that she hadn't eaten anything at all yet that day. *Order some food first*, she decided, and *then you can reach out to Amelia. Got to get moving on this.*

Mia tried to imagine what she would say to this other woman. *Obviously she meant something more to you than the others,* she told Burton. The other models had been hidden safely, locked inside his computer, while the Polaroid of Amelia had swum around inside his underwear drawer. *Such an intimate place,* Mia noted.

Don't read that much into it, ghost Burton tried to assure her. She rolled her eyes at him. *Hey, I just really liked that picture,* he protested, shrugging his shoulders sheepishly. If he had been there, Mia imagined that she might punch his arm or throw the photograph at him to protest his making light of her fears. She was surprised at how the anger bubbled up so quickly again inside of her. She set down her Yakisoba noodles, which were still in their takeout container. Then she stabbed the food with her chopsticks. A piece of chicken flew out of the box and landed on her white bedspread. Mia frowned in that way that her mother had always grimaced when Mia had acted out as a child.

Mia had been encouraged by both of her parents to ride horses as a child, to write thank you cards after receiving gifts, to accept dates as a teenager—but only if the dates were arranged between them and the potential suitor's parents. Sometimes one of her parents would come along, or they'd request that the boy join them for a family dinner. Otherwise the date would need to occur in a very public place, and a strict curfew would be enforced.

Her younger sister, Xanthe, had a propensity to sneak out and break other house rules, but Mia liked to make her parents feel proud and secure. When she had acted out, it had mostly been before puberty had hit. When she had been a young child, Mia had always tried to run through the neighborhood with her brothers and their friends, taking off her shirt as they had all done. She had just wanted to scream and run around topless as if she and her friends were wild animals in nature.

Her mother had abhorred this behavior. She would start off giving Mia a warning, but it would quickly escalate to revoking Mia's privileges for the rest of the day, if she caught Mia running through the neighborhood shirtless. Her father wouldn't even look at her or mention it later, after he came home from work and joined her and her mother and siblings at the dinner table. Mia was the oldest of many children already when she was just eight years old. She knew from the looks in both of her parents' eyes that she was meant to set a good example for her brothers and her sister.

Mia's father had always seemed to be off working, and even when he was home for dinner, he had been distant. When Mia got older, if her dad was designated as her chaperone for one of her dates, she felt even more awkward, as she sat there between two men who were veritable strangers to her. As much as she wanted to please her mother in order to keep her home life pleasant, she also longed for her father's approval. She reasoned that if she knew how to make her father proud, she would know something about him, would feel closer to him.

When she and Burton met in her mid-twenties, Mia had found that she was still clinging to this pathetic, desperate need to appease her parents. They had had a whirlwind courtship, but it had still been important to Mia that she and Burton had her parents' blessing. Like a gentleman, Burton had asked Mia's father first for her hand in marriage. Mia had been relieved when he consented, when both of her parents relayed that they loved Burton. If there was still a wild streak inside of Mia, Burton could tame it, she knew her mother must have reasoned.

What would you think now, if you knew? she asked her parents, who were also both deceased now. *Would you say anything, if you could see me now, eating dinner in bed before the sun has even set? Would you feel disillusioned to know that Burton had secrets? Would you be disappointed in me for wanting these women he photographed?*

Or would you just hold me?

11. November 27
(earlier that day)

The French painter used the basement of his home in Bellevue as an artist's studio. Amelia had taken a Lyft to his place from her hotel room in Seattle, after a decadent breakfast in bed, courtesy of the photographer she had worked with the night before. He had put her up in a luxurious Victorian hotel in the Queen Anne neighborhood and, as per their routine, they had taken turns spanking each other while a timer helped the camera to capture all their movements. Amelia got the room for the whole weekend (and room service!) all for the couple of hours she had spent with the sadomasochist, whom she referred to (in her phone contact list or while talking with Emma) as Egregious George. She had found him to be quite the opposite of egregious, but he presented his work online as dark and irreverent.

"When are you shooting with EG again?" Amelia texted Emma during her Lyft ride to Bellevue. "He said that he misses you." Emma texted back that she would be in Seattle soon after Amelia got home, as was often the case.

"Well, I guess it will be my turn to miss you. Wine and pizza after you get back?" she suggested. Emma shot back that she'd love to, and wished Amelia a good day at work.

Amelia would see Natalia later on during her weekend visit, on Sunday, which promised to be slower than the hustle and bustle of Saturday. Natalia and Amelia enjoyed having wine together any time they were in the same town. Amelia could never convince the tiny model to join her for pizza or dessert, but she could always count on Emma. Still, she looked forward to seeing them both soon. She was nearing Julian's home, according to GPS. Amelia had found him on *Model Mayhem*, not through either of her model friends, but she smiled when she tried to imagine either of her friends sitting for a painter.

Natalia and Emma both had so much natural energy. Amelia did too, but she somehow knew how to rein it in and focus. Natalia needed to be bouncing around the room, and Emma required a constant stream of sound from internet, radio, or TV; otherwise, she would hum throughout an entire session.

Amelia scolded herself for being judgmental. She also felt like bouncing around rooms most of the time, and she preferred having music on at photo shoots too. But posing for a painter or a sketch artist, something that required her to sit very still for long periods of time, was one of the only ways she had found she could meditate. She always looked forward to rushing away from her busy routine to sit still for someone.

Her Lyft driver pulled his car into Julian's driveway, and she felt a wave of fear descend upon her as she imagined entering a new collaborator's home. She shook it off as she remembered how much she had admired his work online and had seen other models revere him in the comments section of his page. They had all hailed him as professional and respectable. She climbed out of the car and walked up the front steps toward his home, and then knocked on the front door.

Without taking very long to come to the door, Julian opened it and introduced himself. He had dark blond hair, which was fine on both his scalp and in his mustache. He was average height and his body was fit, no love handles poking out from his classic, fitted white tee. Amelia gave her name as "Margot" even though she had recently begun to struggle with identifying as Margot. She thought more of Margot as a product she had invented, and was often tempted to talk about her in the third person, but she knew that would sound pretentious or insane.

Julian led her down to the studio. It had been converted and finished well. It was pristine and there was a slight chill to the air, but it wasn't frigid. Amelia took off her coat, but the rest of her clothing remained on. She had posed for many figure studies before, and she felt excited that only her head would be painted today. The painter explained that he would focus mainly on her face but would bring a bit of the collar of her aquamarine sweater into the painting as well. "I like that shade of blue," he explained. Julian told Amelia that she could ask for a break at any time. She nodded eagerly, anticipating the quiet meditation that was imminent.

With four hours ahead of them, Amelia wondered how long she could go before requesting a break. Julian broke down first, after moving his brush swiftly for nearly an hour. Amelia was surprised to learn that much time had elapsed already. She had been focusing her gaze on one of Julian's finished paintings, which hung on the wall to the left of where he was seated. Her mind had been flooded by the myriad emotions that she felt Julian was trying to convey through all the different shades he had applied to his subject's face. She had contemplated that array of emotions until her mind had finally gone blank.

When Julian suggested a break, Amelia stood up to use the restroom. When she returned, he said to her, "Margot, your hair is different than in your portfolio."

"Oh yeah, sorry, I should have warned you about that," she replied with a slight flush to her face. She ran her fingers through her hair nervously. In addition to being shorter, the blue dye had all rinsed out and left her with blonde locks. She had been so busy that she'd forgotten to do something about it. Amelia didn't care much for conventional hair colors, and had been planning to go purple next.

"No, I love it!" Julian exclaimed, his eyes following her as she roamed his room. "You remind me of Mia Farrow," he added. His eyes moved down from her hair to take in her exuberant smile. After her smile faded from a half moon to a sliver, Amelia proceeded to wander the room some more, staring into Julian's paintings and then out of his windows.

Mixing some more blues and greens with his white paint, Julian waited until he had the hues blended to his satisfaction, and then invited Amelia to sit and pose again. She came quickly to assume the position again, deftly angling her body to just the right degree, her gaze fixed in the same spot. She listened to Julian's brush move back and forth as her mind quieted itself again.

After bringing her a glass of water on their next break, Julian asked Amelia a multitude of questions about her life as a freelance model. Amelia respected Julian already, as she admired his work so much. She felt compelled to answer him honestly, then cringed at some of her responses. When he asked if she enjoyed being a model, she said, "Well… I do and I don't."

As he cleaned his brushes, Amelia explained to Julian that she loved posing for people like him, who were creating real art. She had begun to dread working with some of the "fauxtographers," especially if it was someone new, not a regular whom she felt she could trust. She vacillated between calling them fauxtographers, rich weirdos, or, as she explained to Julian, the ever-present label of supreme judgment in the industry, "guys with cameras."

His eyes widened with curiosity and amusement, and he asked her to elaborate. She described the guys with cameras as typically older men, retired or white collar, married, divorced, widowed (never just single), who possessed the money and the impetus to hire young(ish), pretty (enough) women under the guise of creating art or helping them develop their fashion portfolios. What they were uniformly bereft of was an artistic eye. "More often than not," she added, "they spend more time talking, less time shooting. They just want someone to spend time with, really."

Julian admitted that he was surprised to hear that the amateur photographers seemed to share this duplicitous intention. But Amelia assured him, "It doesn't offend me. It just … becomes almost a different job than the one I originally signed up for." She explained that she had found it fairly benign at first, and she had compassion for these men, and that helped her to get through, now that her excitement about what she had gleaned as an easy moneymaking endeavor began to wane. She fell silent, worried about appearing unprofessional.

"It sounds like a very interesting line of work," Julian offered, and she smiled gratefully, and agreed that it was.

"I just really enjoy making real art, or contributing to it, you know?" Julian nodded in agreement.

Naturally they grew quiet as they prepared to get back into the piece. Amelia derived a basic sense of satisfaction whenever she could help someone, and she realized that, after discovering some of the men she would work for weren't all that interested in photography, she had justified it to herself by thinking of the harmless way in which she would help these lonely men. But over time, her reserves of patience and her energy were gradually drained as she came to dread these encounters. She knew there would be so much fake laughter, so much forced smiling that her face would ache after a "shoot," that she would feel drained after simply hanging out in her lingerie next to a strange man for half a day, being devoured by his hungry eyes.

Perhaps that was why Amelia had made the segue into pornography: to shorten the encounter. People did not take long to reach their orgasms—at least Amelia had found that this was true for the small handful of people she had slept with on camera. She remembered that had been the draw for Emma, when she had begun to shoot harder scenes. But Amelia knew that there was more to her own decision than that. She had initially been drawn to making porn because she would be working with her girlfriends, women with whom she slept in real life. Therefore, she had believed, she would be able to showcase real girl-on-girl sex and authentic female orgasms. *This is my girlfriend. I am not posing in an expression of female sexuality that was half-baked inside some guy's brain,* she used to tell herself proudly when she had first decided to embark on that adventure, and had prepared to hold her proverbial shield against the thoughts and opinions of viewers and critics.

Now she realized it wasn't as real as she had intended it to be. Emma and Natalia both had boyfriends, and neither could seem to imagine themselves in a real relationship with a woman. Amelia used to sleep with them off camera; now she only slept with them for money. Now Amelia felt like a fraud.

It was hard for her to wrap her head around the fact that she had started out with the intention to work only as a fashion and art model. A couple of years after high school had ended, back when she had posed for her friend Adele, she had held a red apple and pouted like a tortured, gothic Snow White. She loved to remember that image, how they had created something with a message. They had had a vision they were trying to convey. What did Amelia want to express now?

Julian called for another break and Amelia got back to talking with him right away. She felt a fondness for him that was different from the softness she felt for some of the wannabe sugar daddies for whom she posed: Amelia admired Julian as an artist. She didn't feel a warmth toward him that was derived from pity. Perhaps they were equals, and in Amelia's interactions with the rich weirdos, she felt she had the upper hand: they had the money, but she possessed something that they wanted even more.

Julian expressed that he was impressed with Amelia's ability to travel all over and make money from different creative endeavors. She admitted that she felt like a fraud, wanting to be a model but posing for Guys with Cameras. Julian paused before divulging, "I feel like a fraud, too. I feel like a *Guy with a Brush*."

His face flushed while Amelia chuckled and tried to help him shake off his own insult. "No, you're amazing! You're actually an insanely talented artist!" she assured him. He touched the end of his brush to his lower lip, plotting his next brush stroke, and the action somehow reminded Amelia of Diego. Her wild abandon toward Diego in turn led her to think about Lila, her reckless behavior in following Lila around the Pearl District that day.

"Maybe everyone feels like a fraud sometimes," Amelia suggested to Julian. She was thinking of poor Lila, often revered for her feminist art but always shrinking from the limelight. She had confided in Amelia that whenever she was awarded accolades or invited to interview for local, national, even foreign press, she felt undeserving. *Imposter syndrome*. Amelia told Julian how talented Lila was, how she was a revolutionary in her genre. Julian confessed that he was also a feminist and was intrigued by the description of Lila's work.

As they began to settle in for the final hour, Amelia sat up straighter, squared her shoulders, and fixed her gaze on the distance again. Her mind replayed so many moments from the last five years spent modeling full time. She thought about how many times she had been nervous in a new photographer's "studio" (usually their garage or living room or some other part of their home, or a rented hotel room). She thought of how she had to employ the use of drugs to make herself feel comfortable sleeping with Sam, or even Natalia, who had always encouraged Amelia to bring some cocaine to their shoots as sort of a mental lubricant for them both. Amelia hadn't needed it at first, she had told herself. But she had been on molly that first time she slept with Natalia. Their first time was off screen, but Amelia had been nervous to sleep with a virgin of sorts, a woman who had never been with another woman before. Natalia said that she had enjoyed the molly, but she preferred coke.

Amelia thought hard to remember the last time she had slept with someone without money or drugs being involved, but she stopped trying after she couldn't recall anything in the past year.

As the sadness crept in, her face felt naked. She had been so fearless when she had first started out in the industry, so certain that she had been in control. She was the author of her own sexy choose-your-own-adventure. She was both the navigator and the pilot. The skies had been clear as she had taken off. But now it was filled with thick clouds.

A teardrop threatened to fall. Amelia felt protective of her tough girl image, as if Margot were her little sister or her daughter. *Someday maybe you can share these salty tears with someone, but it will be on your own terms,* her superego whispered to her id.

The painter asked her when she would be back in town, and if she could return for another four-hour session so he could finish the piece. She informed him that she would be back in exactly one month and she agreed to return to his studio. Hesitantly, she asked him if she could see what he had done so far. "Please, please!" he said, motioning for her to come around to the other side of the canvas to see the piece.

Amelia loved seeing the hard bones of her face softened by lighter hues on top of the tan base that he had started off with. Her hair was a partially-filled-in pale yellow halo. Her mouth and her gaze looked pensive.

Feeling revived, Amelia told Julian she was looking forward to working with him again. She couldn't wait to come alive in his vision. He offered her a ride to her next gig, so that she wouldn't have to order another Lyft, and she accepted his offer. She had a pinup shoot to get to, which would be followed by a bondage shoot. She climbed into Julian's car: she had little time to waste, and no fear of him.

12. November 29

Amelia snorted a fat line through a plastic straw with her eyes closed. After a long train ride back to Portland, she had originally planned to take the rest of the night off, to recover from the trip. She was exhausted. But Emma had texted while she was on her way back, and had offered her a last-minute shoot for two hundred dollars. *Easy hour,* Emma had promised. *We can fake it.* Since they were no longer lovers in real life, Emma had taken to hovering over Amelia when she was on top, never putting her mouth all the way onto Amelia. Amelia could always feel her friend's breath, swore it gave her blue clit. She was surprised at how tired she was from her short trip to Seattle and Bellevue, and how burnt out on modeling for Guys With Cameras she was already; how weary she was growing of having sex on camera with women she had once enjoyed, like Natalia, or faking the sex scenes with Emma. So Amelia sucked in a big hit of the coke to keep herself awake.

Only a few short moments later, there was a rush of cold that quickly turned into a warmth spreading down her body. Her limbs felt tingly, but it was a while before she began to tremble from the strong cocaine. A numbness settled over her mind, a pleasant fog. She wanted to hear Lana.

Lana Del Rey often provided the soundtrack to her downward spiral. *Been trying hard not to get into trouble, but I've got a war in my mind,* she sang inside Amelia's head.

Amelia got into the playlist called *This is Lana* on her internet radio, and after she heard the first dark, low note, she turned it up, and anticipated the brightness that would follow as the singer's voice climbed to a more youthful timbre. She looked over at Emma, who was unfazed. Emma didn't care what was playing, but she liked rap music the most. What was important to Emma was just that any sounds permeated the air and covered the mysterious silences.

Emma didn't care for drugs, but she didn't mind if Amelia did them around her. A chill spread up Amelia's back and through her hair as she came up a little more. She ran her hands through her hair. She threw her head back and when she straightened, she saw that Emma was offering her a drink. Sweet Emma, always the caretaker for her friends. It was a side that Amelia knew not everyone got to see.

Her feet rubbed up against each other, against Amelia's will: she was restless. *I just ride,* Lana sang. Amelia rode the wave of the high, clutching onto it.

Emma poured herself a glass of the same champagne that she had offered Amelia. They were going to shoot girl-girl at Emma's place, and were waiting for the photographer to arrive. Emma didn't usually like to have photographers over, especially if her boyfriend might be home, but he was out, and she felt comfortable with the man who would be shooting them. Emma had shown Amelia some examples of the photographer's work earlier, and he purported to have a mission much like Lila Fox's: to capture raw, authentic, female sexuality. Therefore, Emma explained, the photographer, Max, would only shoot girl-on-girl, or a man going down on a woman, or a woman playing with herself. Amelia chuckled over how these definitions of "real female sexuality" were so arbitrary.

When he arrived, Amelia noticed how much younger he was than the stereotypical pornographer. Max was tall, slender, and had long, greasy hair. He wore glasses and a t-shirt that read "The Future Is Female." Amelia stood up to shake his hand and then got light-headed from the coke, sitting back down on Emma's cushy couch immediately. Emma, always eager to get straight to business, asked Max for directives.

Max was soft-spoken as he explained what he had in mind for the evening. "I was thinking, I'd actually just like the two of you to try out this idea I've had for a while: If you're up for it, I'd like to have the two of you play *Dance Dance Revolution* while naked."

Amelia and Emma exchanged a look, psychically checking in with each other. Amelia smirked, and Emma shrugged. Amelia asked Max skeptically, "That's it? That's all you want?" *No fake sex?*

"Yeah," he assured them. "And I'll still pay you each two hundred dollars for the hour, of course."

Amelia smiled a genuine smile then. *Sometimes this job isn't so bad,* she thought. She turned off Lana so that they would be able to hear the dance music in the video game. She and Emma stripped as Max set up his tripod, and then Emma turned on her TV and video game console.

The two women laughed as they struggled to mimic each move they saw on the screen. Sometimes they bumped into one another and giggled harder. The champagne and coke had gone straight to Amelia's head, making everything even more hilarious. She couldn't remember the last time they had laughed this much or this hard, and she reveled in the moment.

After they finished playing their game and collected their pay, Amelia began to pack up her things.

"Oh, I meant to tell you earlier about this woman who wants to meet up and talk with you," Emma told her.

"Oh yeah? Sounds promising," Amelia teased, imagining it was another model.

"Yeah, some photographer's wife. You knew her husband. You know, Burton?" Emma said.

Amelia felt her eyebrows knit together. "*Knew* him?"

Emma looked into Amelia's eyes and then tossed her head back, rolled her eyes at herself, then met Amelia's gaze again. Her eyes were pools of sorrow and sympathy then. "Yeah, you know, um… he died."

Amelia had received the news about Burton too late to attend his funeral, so she decided to have her own memorial for Burton, on some night when she could find time to eat an elegant meal and have an expensive glass of wine or some scotch. Or both.

The opportunity presented itself when Amelia was back in Bellevue a couple of weeks later, to sit for Julian again so that he could finish his painting. Bellevue, the snooty older cousin of Seattle, had nothing but posh places to dine in. Amelia picked one that was near her hotel room and had a fire pit out back, so that she could sit outside and smoke after dinner if she felt like it. The restaurant was dimly lit and every surface that she could see, from the exposed kitchen to the bar, was sleek. Everyone was dressed smart and all the items on the menu were priced a few dollars higher than they should have been. *Burton,* Amelia knew, *would have liked it here.*

Thinking of all the older photographers she knew with their various health problems—cancer, heart failure, strokes—she shook her head. She remembered many times feeling a fondness for them, if they weren't too salacious or smug, too interested in talking about themselves, as a Guy with a Camera was wont to do. On many occasions, Amelia had felt a pull toward a sweet old man, if he struck her as avuncular, and then she instantly felt the urge to fight against that pull, as she thought to herself, *Who knows how much longer he is going to live?*

Amelia rolled her eyes at herself and felt herself frowning. *And here one of my youngest regulars is gone.*

Strangely enough, that was when she got the email from Mia. Amelia had meant to turn her ringer off when she sat down to dinner, but had forgotten, so when she heard her phone make the sound that signified she had a new email message, she couldn't resist the temptation to look, figuring that it was about a shoot.

"Damn," she mumbled aloud, seeing the sender's name listed as *Mia Hughes*. Amelia opened it anyway. She let out a frustrated moan, as she had been hoping to spend this night alone with Burton, or at least with her thoughts on Burton. *How like a wife to barge in on that*, Amelia joked to herself. Mia's email was a breathless, run-on sentence that implored Amelia to meet soon.

Amelia felt for her. She remembered Burton's reveries, how often he had sung Mia's praises, his eyes filled with pure love. *How could something so real just end?* Amelia wondered.

It was a Wednesday evening, and Amelia wrote back that she could get together on Friday afternoon. Mia wrote back almost immediately and confirmed that the date and time would work for her. Amelia noticed that Mia had offered to compensate her for her time, but Amelia ignored that and told Mia what part of town she'd be in on Friday, asked if she could join her for a drink at her favorite French restaurant, Le Pichet. Amelia couldn't eat anything there now that she was vegan, but she had enjoyed the atmosphere so much when she had first discovered it that she often returned just for a drink.

Amelia turned her phone off then and decided she'd look for a confirmation on Thursday. She wanted to enjoy the rest of her evening, her memories of Burton. She thought to herself that coming to Seattle would never be the same, because she wouldn't be able to work with Burton, or share a drink and talk with him about art and travel. Then another thought came into her mind: perhaps she would always be able to spend time with Burton when she visited Seattle, in the same way that she was spending time with him now.

So she raised her glass of scotch, just a little, not wanting to look like a crazy person as she sat alone in the restaurant. For Burton, her photography hero, was gone but would never truly vanish.

⚭

December 13

A couple days later, while Amelia waited in the French bistro for Mia to arrive, she heard the song *"Ne Me Quitte Pas"* come on the internet radio playing from the restaurant's speakers. She had only heard Nina Simone's rendition before, and now she froze, cold goosebumps spreading up her arms and legs, as she heard a man singing it. His voice wasn't quite as deep as Nina's could be when she went into her lower register, but his delivery was commanding. He went quickly from low and subtle to loud and forceful. She felt as if she were being pushed around by a rough man, maybe a boxer, but then his voice fell to a lilt again and she lost her fear and her thrill, and all she was left with was a feeling of despondency.

As if on cue, Mia walked through the door. Amelia was struck by how perfectly the music fit Mia's lost and disconsolate expression, and the hopeless aura around her gray clothing. She plodded in, wearing sensible boots, and shook the raindrops from her black umbrella. Then she caught Amelia watching her and smiled in a way that seemed almost peculiar to Amelia. It was unexpected and didn't quite fit their situation. But in spite of herself, Amelia returned Mia's grin.

"You must have found my pictures, then?" Amelia asked as Mia sat down across from her.

Mia frowned but Amelia could see a haze in her eyes that implied she was suddenly somewhere else. Then abruptly she snapped out of it, and Mia explained, "I'm sorry, I got distracted by the music, and—your hair is different!" Then she added, "It's nice."

Amelia ran her fingers through her hair. She had just gone to the salon the day before for a trim, to make her pixie cut neater, and had her hair dyed dark purple as well.

Mia looked around the restaurant. "I've never been here. This place is really lovely."

"I love it here," Amelia said, nodding her head. "This music caught me off guard too. I've heard the song, but not this version."

"Oh, that's Jacques Brel," Mia said. "I've always loved the way he sings it. Do you speak French?"

Amelia shook her head.

Mia interpreted the lyrics for her: "He's saying 'Don't leave me.'" They both looked down at the table and sat in silence for a moment.

Amelia noticed the waiter approaching and asked Mia, "Can I get you a glass of wine or something?"

Mia shook her head and gasped. "It's on me, really. I insist. I'm just so grateful that you could meet with me. By the way, you never told me how much you wanted in the way of…*compensation*," she said, her voice hushed as she spoke her last word.

"I couldn't charge you anything. I am just so sorry for your loss and also sorry for, well, this sort of bombshell that came after," Amelia explained. Mia's eyes began to water a little. Amelia wanted to push for buying the drinks, but she worried she would sound like she was pitying Mia too much. Amelia despised being pitied herself.

"Thanks. It really *was* a bombshell. I mean, I knew that he liked to shoot landscapes and portraits, but I had no idea that he was taking pictures of nude women. And so many of them!" Mia exclaimed, and then she looked around the room in embarrassment, lowering her voice again on the last word that escaped her mouth.

When the waiter stopped by their table, Mia ordered a glass of bordeaux, and Amelia said she'd like the same. Mia instructed the waiter to put them both on her tab.

They fell into another silence for a while. It wasn't exactly awkward, but it was filled with so much palpable uncertainty, which Amelia knew was coming from both of them.

Finally Mia broke the silence: "I guess what I mainly wanted to ask you was… What was your relationship like with my husband exactly?" Mia's eyes showed her truth: that she really did want to know the whole story, despite any pain she may incur in hearing it.

The waiter dropped off their drinks and asked if they would like anything to eat. Neither of the women were hungry.

Amelia took a sip from her glass of wine before she answered. "He was the most professional photographer I ever worked with. I felt safe around him every time we shot, and he was…he was so in love with you," she said. She watched Mia's eyes soften and grow teary, but she continued. "He sang your praises all the time. I wasn't interested in anything more than working with him and maybe being friends. I never would've tried anything with him, but it really wouldn't have mattered either way. He never would have given in to my advances, even if I had tried."

Mia's face was beaming with gratitude. "I just don't know why he hid this…passion from me. I thought that if he felt the need to shoot nude photography and kept that from me, that maybe there was even more that he was hiding," she explained.

"That's understandable," Amelia said. "But I never met a man who seemed more married than Burton."

They grew quiet again, each sipping from their wineglasses. Finally Mia posed another question: "Do you often feel unsafe? Do men make passes at you, at photo shoots?"

Amelia laughed bitterly. "You wouldn't believe how often," she replied. "But a lot of times it's passive-aggressive. Like, they won't really proposition me, but they'll keep complimenting my looks and they can get away with it because, well, they're staring at my body, so I think, 'Well, what else do we have to talk about?' And then they might mention other arrangements they have made with different models, trying to test the waters. It's exhausting, feeling like I'm a bone in a dog's face all day."

"I can imagine that that would be," Mia exclaimed. "Has anything bad ever happened to you at one of your jobs?"

"No. I've been lucky to just be creeped out, mostly," Amelia responded. Then after she thought about it some more, she added, "Well, there was this one time: I had a bondage shoot and we had negotiated all of the terms ahead of time. It usually works out well if you're just upfront about everything that you're OK with and everything that you aren't. But after this guy tied me up, he cut my shirt off without letting me know that he was planning to do that or asking if it was all right to destroy my shirt. And he scraped my chest a little bit with the scissors. Then he sprayed me with cold water from a spray bottle, and it was really uncomfortable. He ended that scene and untied me. I was standing up at that point, and had just my hands tied back. Then he said he wanted to tie me down to the bed, spread-eagle, and I said no. Fortunately he listened and we ended the shoot and he still paid me. Maybe he felt bad for scaring me."

"As he should," Mia said. She shook her head in disbelief. Mia's eyes were so lovely to Amelia when they were wide with concern. Her long hair shaking in big, loose waves made Amelia want to run her fingers through it.

She liked that Mia's body was curvier than her own. Mia appeared soft but strong. Amelia could see why Burton had been so enamored with his wife.

Mia took a swallow of her drink and then found that her glass was empty. "Well," she said to Amelia, with one eyebrow raised, "what next?"

Amelia shook her head a little, smiled with just one side of her mouth. "I don't know." She wasn't sure if Mia meant to ask her what she intended to do with her hopeless career, or if she had intended to make more plans for the two of them now that their wine was gone. But Amelia suddenly felt tired and had some shooting to do early the next day. She thanked the widow, apologized for needing to vanish so suddenly, and then she disappeared.

13. December 13
(later that evening)

The way that Amelia's rosebud mouth would break spontaneously from a pursed expression of concern to a wide stretched smile continued to penetrate Mia's mind after she returned home from their meeting. She knew that her mind was looking for another distraction to ease her heart's pain, but she didn't banish the fantasy that crept in like a spirit, that she might have regarded as an interloper on some other night.

Ordinarily Mia took her showers in the morning. If she bathed at night, it was usually a hot bath with salts and bubbles. But now Mia wanted to stand up. She turned on the water before getting in, so that it would be the perfect temperature by the time she disrobed. She stepped in, and the hot water felt good on her skin as it came down on her.

The room began to fill up with steam, which she enjoyed inhaling. She massaged her skin with a loofah lathered up with body wash. The water rinsed it off just after it foamed. Mia grabbed the shower head from its holder. She conjured up the memory of the first photograph she had ever seen in Amelia's file. It haunted her more than the other images she had seen: the tall, lithe woman, her hair long and baby blue, had gazed up toward the light, her large eyes inviting. Her breasts looked firm and perky, yet soft.

Daydreaming of doing things that she had only seen in TV shows, or in porn, Mia moved the shower head setting so that the water stream would come out harder and more concentrated. She imagined Amelia then, kneeling before her in the shower, looking up with big eyes that conveyed that she longed to please Mia. She looked as if she were waiting for instruction.

"Lick my pussy," Mia whispered.

"Yeah, is that what you want?" Amelia teased.

"Yes," Mia said aloud. "I want you to." Then she aimed the shower head at her clit, holding her lips open with two fingers. She could easily imagine that small mouth of Amelia's softly beginning to open around Mia's clit, her tongue coming through, gently beginning to lick up and down.

Mia took her hand away from her labia, braced herself by placing that hand on the tile wall before her. Her other hand continued to move the shower head up and down in small but precise movements. Unconsciously she began rocking her hips. Then she began to imagine Amelia slipping a finger inside of her, fucking Mia with her finger while sucking on her clit.

It was more than Mia could stand, or so she thought. Amelia carefully began to add a second finger, paying attention to Mia's body to see if she was ready. Once she had slid the second finger in, she began fucking her harder, and her tongue moved in perfect rhythm with her hand.

Mia began groaning. She imagined grasping Amelia by the hair, holding her head in place so that she could finish now. "I'm going to come on your face!" Mia warned her.

"Yeah," Amelia cried in excitement. "I want to taste you."

Mia came so hard that her legs trembled afterward. She had to move the shower head away immediately as she grew too sensitive for any more stimulation. She slid down until she was sitting on the wet floor of the tub, taking long, deep breaths to recover.

After she collected herself, she stood and grabbed a towel to dry herself off with. When she was dry and had finished combing her hair, she headed to the bedroom. She lay down and clutched a pillow as if it were a lover to hold, and she fell asleep quickly, imagining that a soft woman was nestled close to her.

14. December 15

The end of Amelia's Seattle-area visit was marred by a revelation from Natalia: she had decided to quit the business. She had been seeing her boyfriend for what seemed like an eternity, but they had only just begun to settle into his home as Natalia had gradually moved out of her bachelorette pad in Seattle. The boyfriend lived in Bothell, a suburb near Seattle, and he was a butcher. He had asked Natalia not only to cohabitate, but he had marriage and babies on his mind, and possibly something more deleterious: he had suggested that Natalia quit modeling, stay at home, and figure out what her "true passion" was.

Amelia could never remember the boyfriend's name. *Who cares?*

Now she longed to feel happy for her friend, and not suspicious. But whenever a man offered to support a woman financially, Amelia felt dubious of his intentions. She knew that this stemmed from her own upbringing, with a mother who had mostly stayed single, after fleeing with Amelia from her own father. He was a controlling man, "financially abusive," they said. Not *just* financially abusive, they also said. She didn't remember much about him, but he frowned in every memory she could conjure up. He was tall and thick, his lips perpetually downturned, and the knowledge of his proclivities lent a dark shadow to his being every time she thought of him. Her mother had taken her and left her father when Amelia was just seven years old. She knew her mother had been poor, young, and afraid, and she felt so proud whenever she imagined her mother at that crossroads, making the final decision to leave the man who had provided for her and her child.

What had he provided, really? Money, security, health insurance? Cracks to her mother's self-esteem, holes in the walls. *Bruises on my mother.*

"He never laid a hand on me, if that's what you're thinking," Amelia would have told people, to dissuade them from ascribing that old cliche to her. She was not perpetuating some kind of abuse on herself by choosing to share her body with the world.

Insecure now in how she felt about some of the directions she had gone in, where she would go next, Amelia still knew that her expression of sexuality was a bold, political act, and that she had opportunities to share authentic expressions of sexuality as art. It did not come from some scarring event in her childhood, some man touching her. Had a man touched her? Not in childhood. Had a man ever harassed her, or touched her against her will, or made her feel afraid or unsafe in her adulthood? Hell yes, but what woman could say that these things had not happened to her, at least once in her life?

"My father left when I was young. He had no impact on my work. He left before he could really do me any harm," Amelia would have told people, if she had felt the need to defend her choices and her projects. But she didn't.

Over a glass of wine in a little cafe near the waterfront in downtown Seattle, Natalia was telling Amelia everything was over.

It had been a while since they had had sex outside of work, anyway. Amelia hadn't expected that to happen again after they had settled into their routine of working and then going out for wine afterwards, talking about the boyfriend, talking like girlfriends, but not *girlfriends*. But now, there would be no more photo shoots, no more cocaine, no more wine, and probably a lot fewer nights out. Natalia wouldn't travel to Portland to shoot with her anymore, and stay the night and get wasted. Of course, she would still see Amelia when Amelia came to Seattle. Natalia promised this, but Amelia knew that they might have perfunctory, awkward conversations over tea, as Natalia had said that she would soon have to abstain from wine and coffee as she prepared her body for pregnancy. They certainly wouldn't have their nights out, dancing on coke anymore.

At least Amelia would no longer have to struggle with her mixed feelings about sleeping with Natalia. It had begun to nag at her subconscious: why would she have sex with women who said that it didn't "really count"? Was that empowering, or healthy for Amelia's self-esteem?

"What will you do with your free time, besides…trying to grow a baby?" Amelia asked Natalia, taking a big swig of pinot gris. It burned a little as she poured too much down her throat, but it helped to shake her from her shock over the news of Natalia's early retirement.

Natalia smiled a shy smile as she confessed, "I've been doing pottery, ceramics, stuff like that. I think I will continue to make things, try to sell them online, you know? Maybe eventually I could have a booth at the Pike Place Market."

Amelia nodded and tried to convey ebullient support of her friend's new dream while assuaging the doubts that she knew were merely born of her own biases. If nothing else, Amelia was self-aware. She rolled her eyes at herself mentally. *Just because you don't want to be sitting at some booth on some cold day in the Northwest, trying in vain to sell the creations that you labored over, that were meant to express deeply personal feelings but come across obscure to some on the glossy, ceramic surface…*

Natalia appeared happy with her decision, and Amelia felt that it was important to cheer all her friends on. Unless their boyfriends crossed a line, in which case a different responsibility trumped the former. Amelia ordered champagne next and convinced Natalia to stay out a little later, finish the bottle with her. She raised her glass in a toast to her friend, hoping desperately that they would settle into a new routine that still involved texting and visiting one another.

In all her friendships, the communication waxed and waned. For Amelia, it was mainly her busy schedule that was to blame. For some of her friends, there was simply a lack of follow-through, but Amelia mainly kept in touch with reliable people. For others, there was an intimacy issue at play, which was undoubtedly the case with Amelia's old friend Ginger.

Ginger was a redhead, and Amelia had always had a penchant for redheads. Ginger was also the fiercest, most openly polyamorous pansexual Amelia knew. Ginger could have taken the same route that Amelia and her other girlfriends had taken and made a foray into modeling or making videos. She had certainly expressed an interest whenever Amelia talked about her fetish projects or the piles of money she was making. Ginger was a self-described fiend for bondage and pain. It didn't even matter to her whether she was the top or the bottom in the situation, as long as she was involved in some kind of BDSM role play.

The reason Ginger had never asked Amelia for any contacts was that she was simply not confident about her looks. She was average in height, thin, and had small breasts. Everything about her was tiny except for her hopeful yet discerning eyes, which were like two saucers on her child-size face. Ginger's skin was creamy, not pale like Amelia's. Amelia admired Ginger's creamy skin and Emma's tan skin as she lusted after these palettes for herself. But sadly, even when Amelia got to visit a warm place, the tans never seemed to last long after she returned to the bleak Northwest.

Ginger talked about wanting to be a bondage model, but whenever Amelia offered to put Ginger in touch with photographers, she always shook off the suggestion, saying her tits were too small. Her stomach was too saggy. Her butt was too droopy. None of these things were true. Ginger had children and Amelia knew that many women lamented that things just weren't in the same place any longer on their bodies after they gave birth and breastfed. Amelia met Ginger after she had already started having kids. She couldn't imagine Ginger's body looking any more svelte though.

Amelia left Seattle on a flight to Chicago, where she would stay with Ginger. Ginger had offered to be a bodyguard for her at her shoot, since Amelia had not met the photographer in person yet. Amelia took her up on this, and as she sat on the plane in first class (courtesy of the photographer she would soon meet), she looked forward to having time with Ginger at the shoot and outside of her work that weekend.

Having recently left her husband of several years, Ginger was in an open relationship with the owner of a small bookstore. "The kids will be with their dad this weekend," Ginger texted Amelia before she arrived in Chicago. Amelia replied, "Cool." Not that she minded the children being around, in general, but for a person without kids, the trysts she had had with Ginger in the past were hot when they were alone together in the bedroom at night, but the mornings after were slightly awkward with toddlers running in and trying to jump on the bed.

They had originally met in Portland when Ginger had owned her own craft shop there. She eventually sold it and moved to the Midwest with her husband, when they were still married, so that they could be closer to all their relatives. Now she was a single mother in a rough city, so naturally she had initially worried about support. Her ex had seemed to inherit all their relatives and old friends: he had gotten them all on his side during their acrimonious divorce. But Ginger was like a cat: she always landed on her feet. She made friends easily in Chicago just as she did everywhere. She had the bookstore owner boyfriend, and now, she said, all she needed were some close girlfriends.

Now that she was selling vintage clothing online, Ginger set her own schedule and said it was no problem for Amelia to come visit whenever she wanted, and to stay as long as she desired.

Ginger picked her up from the O'Hare Airport. She had a deep-dish pizza waiting in the back of the car for Amelia. "I figured you would be hungry, so I got you a deep dish, even though I still don't understand why you like it," Ginger teased.

"Oh no!" Amelia exclaimed, and then she turned red as she thought of how to decline the pizza more graciously. "I'm sorry, it's just that… I'm vegan now," she explained.

"Oh man!" Ginger yelled, turning the steering wheel to exit the passenger pickup lane. "You're always talking about eating pizza!"

"Yeah, but … I mean, *vegan* pizza," Amelia said lightly. She felt so bad that she thought of eating the pie just to be polite, but the thought of veering from her strict diet *and* moral code made her feel nauseous.

Ginger looked at Amelia as if she could sense her inner tumult, and she laughed. "Don't worry about it! It was cheap!" She shook Amelia's left shoulder a little, playfully, and then adapted a cheesy fake Italian accent. "It's cheap pizza, fuhgeddaboudit!"

Amelia laughed and shrugged off her guilt. "So what do you want to do tonight?" she asked Ginger. The clock inside Ginger's car read 8:12 PM.

"Oh, I just figured that you would be tired, after flying for so long," Ginger said.

"No, I'm weird, I don't really get tired from traveling. It energizes me." Amelia watched out the window as they passed the city center, and she took in the spectacular glow of the millions of city lights.

"Well, I had planned to take you back to my place and have some drinks there and just chill out. Then I thought that tomorrow night we could go out downtown somewhere, and if you wanted to, you could meet Edward."

Edward was the boyfriend. Amelia was interested, but also slightly leery: guys were always excited when their girlfriends wanted to bring Amelia over. They heard about her brazen bisexuality, her work in the adult film industry. But it never seemed to lead to a threesome. Amelia sensed that her attraction to women and the attention she paid them seemed to put off every boyfriend or husband she had been set up with. Guys wanted the third partner to be into their partner just enough, not more than they liked men, and not enough to be a threat to them.

Amelia had courted Ginger back in their Portland days, and although they had hooked up, they'd never formally dated. Ginger had always wanted it to remain casual. Amelia had not always wanted it that way, as she had fallen hard for Ginger when she had first met her. Now Amelia was in the same place Ginger had always been in: she liked the simplicity of her relationship with Ginger, whom she could hook up with whenever they were in the same town, and they could go long periods of time forgetting to text each other, without any drama.

Still, Amelia worried that something about her always came across as possessive when she liked a woman and was meeting her boyfriend with the idea of a threesome on everyone's minds. Amelia knew from texting with Ginger before their visit that they had all thought about it. It was premeditated but, as Ginger explained when they reached her home, not expected.

When they arrived at Ginger's place, she showed Amelia to the kitchen. Ginger grabbed a couple cans of beer from the fridge, cracked them open. They moved to the living room to sit on the couch, where Ginger began to show her pictures of Edward. His face appeared to Amelia to be the face of an intellectual: furrowed brow, thick eyebrows, the hair on his head slightly graying, long, imposing nose. His eyes, which twinkled with some kind of insight and were creased at the corners, were adorned with glasses that had smart black frames.

Amelia thought that she would not mind being in bed with either of them. Both of them. *Would not mind at all.*

Of course she would have to meet Edward first, in order to be certain. They made plans to have dinner with him the following evening, after Amelia's photo shoot, and from there, Ginger said, they would go see a friend's band play, where they could have some more drinks. Amelia was amenable; she nodded in assent as Ginger chattered on about the things they could do while they were out, and what kinds of things Edward was into in bed, what he was like as a lover. Amelia sipped her cheap beer, enjoying the cool burn as it went down. After hours of reminiscing about their Portland days, they finally fell asleep together in Ginger's soft, comfy bed in the back room of the apartment. As Amelia drifted off into sleep, she imagined that Ginger's children's rooms were somehow vibrating with the silence of their absence. In her mind, the rooms were blank spaces, as Amelia hadn't peered into those realms.

The shoot the next day was as scattered as an amateur vaudeville show, because the photographer, as he'd explained in advance, wanted to explore many themes. They shot fashion, artistic (in the photographer's opinion, anyway) nudity, pinup, and spanking. Ginger sat in Amelia's place while she touched up her makeup and the photographer adjusted the light, testing it on Ginger. Amelia peeked out of the changing room to see her friend standing in for her, and it endeared Ginger even more to her. She slipped her iPhone out of the pocket of the overalls that she was about to pose topless in, and took a covert shot of Ginger, who sat on a large wooden crate, face in profile from Amelia's perspective, facing the photographer head-on. Ginger had excellent posture as she sat and waited, and perhaps that could have been chalked up to nerves, but she looked perfectly at home.

Amelia made her way back into the scene. After posing in the overalls, the photographer asked Amelia to act out a skit with him, and he switched from the Nikon to a video camera. He enlisted Ginger's help to operate the camera, while he and Amelia acted out his short, supposedly artistic film. Amelia had to leer at the photographer, who was posing as an unsuspecting man in a waiting room, and the scene would culminate in her pulling his pants and underwear down and leaving them like that as she ran out of the room.

Ginger no longer looked perfectly comfortable, but she agreed to operate the camera. She wore a slightly pained expression as she tried to figure out the whole point of the exercise, and gradually her expression progressed from mild disbelief to pure horror. Amelia pulled down the photographer's waistband over and over, as he continued to request that she do it again: he wanted, he said, for his penis to really spring out, almost as if it were making a rubbery "boing" sound. Amelia finally called for a break. Ginger excused herself, "for some fresh air," she said.

The photographer, Mike, looked like a sad clown, minus the makeup and red wig. His body was pear shaped, and his skin was pasty all over. Wiry black hair sprung out randomly across the otherwise bald patches of skin on the parts of his body Amelia had unearthed when she had pulled down his pants. His face was droopy and he was missing quite a few teeth, painfully visible when he tried to force a smile. He wore round, wire-rimmed glasses and had a perfectly smooth bald head. His eyes were as sad as his pouty mouth: they seemed to communicate loneliness, and longing, but also a sense of hopelessness.

Amelia explained to him that she had grown tired of pulling down his pants. She reminded him that she had agreed to do it once, very quickly, and explained that it felt too intimate, doing it repeatedly. He said that he understood, but his face did not seem to convey any understanding. Amelia told him that she didn't usually have much physical contact with the photographers she worked with, but this made him appear further perplexed.

Amelia understood when Mike finally explained that he had seen a video that Amelia was in, where the director had restrained her, whipped her, and then used some toys on her.

"Ahh, yes," she started. "It was all agreed upon in advance. And actually, there still wasn't any skin-to-skin contact happening," she added, a sympathetic but also victorious smile forming on one side of her mouth. Ginger was MIA but Amelia suspected she was probably talking with Edward on the phone, and Ginger confirmed later on that she had been. She had had to run out and tell him how bizarre everything was getting, how she didn't know how to navigate the situation. She had wanted to keep Amelia safe, but Ginger didn't know if Amelia's boundaries had been crossed or not. Amelia told her later that she had done just fine: she would have asked Ginger to stay if she'd needed her.

The photographer asked her to kneel over his lap for the last set. Amelia did as she was instructed to do, and Mike spanked her with his hand. He asked if he could use an object, and they negotiated. When Ginger walked back into the studio, Mike was spanking her friend with a flip-flop.

Discreetly, Amelia sneaked the flip-flop into her bag full of modeling clothes. Later that evening, after the concert, Edward spanked her and Ginger with the same flip-flop. Although Amelia wanted to revel completely in the fact that she finally achieved her first threesome, she got distracted for a brief moment by a new tattoo on Ginger's left hip, which read "*57.*"

Hands on skin, tracing the curves of each other's bodies in the dark, like fingers reading braille. The whole room filled with moans and different aromas: deep, guttural sounds, high breathy sighs, musky, masculine scents, floral, feminine body sprays. Wet spots you can feel no matter which side of the bed you roll onto. The dull ache when two digits go deep inside, almost too deep. Good pain, like the sting of palms and objects slapping your ass.

They loved each other in that moment. Amelia knew that. She also knew that it was transient.

What was important to Amelia? The fact that she was respected. Ginger and Edward had told her what to do, but she knew that it was all part of the game. They had also asked her intermittently if certain things were OK: touching here, biting there? They all fell asleep together, holding on to one another. Amelia had felt loved.

The day after their encounter, Ginger scampered out of her apartment, apologizing to Amelia. She explained on her way out the door that she had to pick up her children and couldn't take Amelia to the airport. "Will it be all right if Edward runs you out there?" Ginger asked her. Amelia shrugged, said it was no problem.

The flatlands of Chicago passed them by as Amelia and Edward sat silent in Edward's clean but antiquated lemon. She imagined that he was searching for some kind of icebreaker to ask her, and she tried to ready herself with some sort of vacuous prattle to fill their long car ride with. Edward surprised her by suddenly bringing up the threesome, explaining how much he had enjoyed it, and how much he thought that Ginger had also enjoyed herself.

"Oh good! It was a lot of fun," she concurred.

As indie rock played from his car stereo, each song more obscure than the next, Edward went on: "Did everything feel OK?" Amelia opened her mouth for a brief second, but Edward kept talking. "I really feel like everyone's boundaries were respected, and everyone got equal amounts of attention, don't you?" Amelia attempted to speak again. "I think it was really the best threesome that I've ever had," Edward said, and then he talked at great length about the other threesomes that he had had, the negative aftermath from a few of them. He talked about how he'd never had one with Ginger before, how Amelia had fulfilled that fantasy for him and Ginger, even though he had had so many threesomes before.

Edward, staring at the road ahead of him through his prescription sunglasses, finally fell silent. Eventually he looked to her for some sort of response, and she just said again, "Yeah. It was a lot of fun."

The next day, via text message, Amelia had to ask her friend what her tattoo meant. It took Ginger several hours to respond but finally she explained that she was Edward's fifty-seventh lover, and that they had a twenty-four/seven sub-dom relationship. He had insisted upon branding Ginger in that way. Really, she didn't mind, or so she said.

Amelia couldn't hold back from expressing what a narcissist Edward seemed like. Ginger admitted that he was, said that he already knew, and was in counseling to try to change. But Ginger liked their relationship, she explained.

"But is he hurting you? In other ways, besides the things you enjoy?" Amelia texted.

Ginger responded, "Nothing we can't work through. He just has a big ego. Sometimes he tells me that he is so much smarter than I am, or how I need to lose weight."

Amelia felt big, fat tears form in the corners of her eyes instantaneously. "Oh Ginger!" she wrote back. "You are so smart, and you are so beautiful! And you don't deserve to hear that."

Did that come out wrong? Amelia wondered. *Put the onus on Ginger?* Edward was the one who needed to feel shitty, in Amelia's opinion. Ginger didn't text back. Amelia worried endlessly.

Amelia, twenty-one hundred miles away, back in Portland now, felt powerless to change the situation. She texted Ginger again, to let her know that she would be there for her any time. Amelia also felt selfishly disappointed in how the experience marred her memory of the threesome. She thought about the time she had watched Lila going into the couple's home. She took out the picture from her underwear drawer. She thought of the male fans she had, finding her email address from her Twitter account where she promoted her work. Many of them paid her for private selfies,

Polaroids, prints, many times admitting that they hid the evidence in their underwear drawers. Now Amelia had joined the ranks.

Pictures she had printed from her digital camera as well as her phone were neatly tucked beneath her socks, and she gathered them in her hands and moved them to her bed. Fanning them out on her bedspread, she made a circle with the pictures, sat and looked at each one. The trampling guy, Lila and her couple, Diego, Ginger… There was also a Polaroid picture she had taken of Natalia doing her makeup before their last kissing fetish shoot. Amelia laughed when she remembered startling Natalia with the sound of the camera snapping the photo and spitting out the image. She remembered how Natalia had always worn a shade of red lipstick with a hint of orange in it at their shoots, which Amelia always had to remind Natalia to wipe off before they began to lock lips. That way, Amelia could avoid looking like a deranged circus clown, red smeared all around her mouth.

Amelia stared at the pictures for a while before realizing she was searching for meaning in these items, and that there was none. They hadn't done much to capture how she felt, and they only reminded her now that she was burnt out and had been seeking a distraction. The encounter with Ginger and Edward felt the same way to her now: it was an experience she had gone into looking for something, some meaning that wasn't there. She had sought out more love, and somehow she had found herself with less. Alone, with no partners, no fulfilling artistic assignments, and her favorite photographer gone, Amelia felt nothing but empty.

After returning her pictures to their hiding place, Amelia put on her boots and coat, and left her apartment for the day. She left her camera behind. She was hungry for something new.

15. December 27

Mia's fantasies about Amelia were like a beacon that she had sent out unconsciously, not expecting that her interest would be returned. She was pleasantly surprised to run into Amelia at Elliot Bay Book Company, not expecting that she would be back in the area again so soon. They had only just had their meeting a couple of weeks earlier, and Amelia had said she usually just came to Seattle once a month. She had resurfaced with new hair: her purple pixie had been dyed black, but Mia couldn't mistake those large cat eyes and tiny freckles on the bridge of her nose. There always seemed to be a twinkle in those eyes that drove Mia crazy. The black tint in Amelia's hair made her skin appear even more milky.

"Amelia! Hi!" Mia started shyly, stopping her in front of the fiction section. Amelia looked somewhat timid as well as she returned Mia's greeting. "What are you doing back so soon?"

"Oh, I got a really good offer, and didn't have much going on back home this week. It's nice to be back again already," Amelia explained. "I was in Tacoma for Christmas, too, to see my mother, so it was nice to pick up a gig over here afterwards, you know, to help pay for the trip. It's sad, though, too, being here and not being able to see..." She trailed off.

Mia nodded, understanding that Amelia was referring to Burton. She shrugged it off, mentally leaning back into her excitement over crossing paths with the model again, as it was a welcome distraction from her grief. "What are you up to?" she asked Amelia.

"I leave tomorrow morning and I finished the book I was reading on my way here, so I needed to get something new." She held *The Essential Neruda: Selected Poems* in her arms.

Mia exclaimed that she loved Pablo Neruda. Amelia smiled at this, and then asked Mia where she was off to next. "Nowhere, no plans really. Are you done with work for the day?" Mia asked, her voice rich with hope.

Amelia nodded and said that she was. "Can I buy you a drink, some dinner?" Mia offered. She could see that Amelia was hesitant, and thought of mentioning that the model would be doing her a favor, but didn't want to guilt her into it, so she decided to remain quiet while Amelia pondered the invitation.

Finally, Amelia replied, "Sure, I'd like that."

The sun had just begun to set as they walked away from the bookstore. Mia was careful to ask Amelia about her dietary restrictions, which seemed to make Amelia smile. Mia chose the restaurant thoughtfully because of Amelia's veganism. As the sky grew dark, snowflakes began to fall around them. Both women smiled brightly like children: it didn't usually snow much in Seattle or Portland, so whenever it did fall it felt a little bit like magic.

They talked with more ease than they had at their first meeting. The restaurant was dark and dimly lit, with soft piano music in the background.

Amelia commented that her tempeh was marinated in some sauce that was delicious. She thanked the widow for the meal. "May I try a bite?" Mia asked, explaining that she had never tasted tempeh before. Amelia nodded and motioned toward the food, inviting her to grab a forkful.

"Mmm!" Mia exclaimed, when the food was on her tongue. After chewing and swallowing, she added, "Tastes so good."

Amelia was happy to see the widow smiling. She couldn't imagine how hard it must have been, being without her husband these last couple months, knowing he would never return home. Mia ran her fingers through her wavy brown locks again, unconsciously calling attention to their shine. The gesture made her want to touch Mia's hair, to run her fingers through it, maybe pull it a little, which made her stifle a tiny smile. Then she frowned, scolded herself internally for lusting after this woman, who was dealing with such an unbearable loss, and who was simply being friendly, taking her out for some food. *Why do you always have to make everything so dirty?* Amelia asked herself.

As they were nearing the end of their meal, Mia ordered two more of what they had each been drinking—scotch, for Burton—and then she covered her face in embarrassment. "I should have asked if you wanted another. I shouldn't have assumed," she cried.

Through her laughter, Amelia assured her that it was all right. "I will rarely turn down a drink," she explained. When the waiter brought their glasses of scotch, they both said, "Cheers," and made their tumblers touch. Mia shared stories about her job, told Amelia she didn't know yet when she would get back to catering. She asked Amelia more about modeling, and her life back in Portland.

Amelia regaled the widow with stories about her travels, as well as her nights out partying with friends. Mia grinned as she tried to imagine living with such wild abandon. Their glasses were empty too suddenly, and seemed to surprise both of the women. "You know, Burton always got the best scotch. I mean, we still have lots." Mia leaned in closer to Amelia over the table. "Have you ever had a sixty-year scotch?" she asked her.

The younger woman chuckled. "Can't say that I have." Her voice betrayed her intrigue. And so she decided then that she should accompany Mia home. She needed to have a taste.

Once inside Mia's home, Amelia noticed right away that it had a very similar feel to the restaurant. Mia turned on low, soothing lights, and Amelia could hear the calming sound of ocean waves in the distance before she saw the view. Everything looked expensive, which didn't surprise Amelia at all. Mia motioned for her to sit on the couch, and Amelia smiled and sat down.

Mia put some jazz on her record player, and Amelia lit up. "Wow, you are so classy!" she exclaimed. Mia blushed in response, feeling old and square, and Amelia giggled. "It's OK," she added, "I have a record player too."

Eyes wide in disbelief, Mia replied, "No, you don't!" She figured she was being teased. Amelia insisted it was true.

"I think albums sound better that way, don't you?" Amelia asked. Mia agreed as she put a glass of scotch in Amelia's hand. They sat quietly for a while, next to each other on the couch, sipping their drinks, savoring them. Suddenly Mia rested her head on Amelia's shoulder. It caught Amelia off guard, but she didn't mind. Then the widow suddenly jerked her head away.

"I'm sorry," she started. "I-I don't know how to do this."

Amelia frowned, puzzled. "Do what?" A long silence filled the room. *Is she trying to come on to me?* Amelia wondered. She hadn't anticipated that, but she wasn't opposed to it. A part of her thought it was inappropriate for her to want Mia, given that she had been Burton's great love. Another part of her felt so drawn to this woman who could understand better than anyone how it felt to miss Burton. Could being with Mia be like being near

Burton again? She felt that it was: being in their home, *their space*, was like being enveloped by his energy. Amelia couldn't resist it any longer.

Lunging forward, she cupped Mia's face with one hand, and leaned in to kiss her lips. Much to her excitement, Mia kissed Amelia back. She enjoyed the way the older woman's lips were fuller than her own, how they seemed to swallow Amelia up. Her head was swimming from the scotch and the intoxicating kisses.

Mia's heart raced as Amelia's hands moved down her body. She put her arms around Amelia and buried her head into her neck, overwhelmed by Amelia's feminine scent. It was like dahlias mixed with burning leaves. She had never been with a woman, but she knew she needed to be with this one.

Amelia pulled back suddenly. "Are you sure this is what you want?" she asked Mia. Mia was quiet for a moment. "I don't want to hurt you," Amelia explained. "I know that this is … a hard time for you." She cringed as she knew that the words didn't match the gravity of her situation.

Now Mia was bold enough to truly make her move, as she couldn't bear the thought of Amelia leaving. She grabbed Amelia by the hips and pulled her closer. There was a line of freckles on Amelia's bare shoulder that Mia wanted to trace. They were like a miniature Orion's belt. She moved her gaze from that constellation back up to Amelia's feline eyes. "Please," she started in a low voice. "I just need to feel…some—" Amelia understood the need Mia was trying to convey. They were both subsumed in darkness, looking for some light together. Before Mia could finish her sentence, Amelia dove back into their kiss.

16. August 13

Mia took her morning coffee outside on the balcony every morning now, while she enjoyed the summer sun's rays. It was August now, the hottest part of the summer in the Northwest, and while some people felt that the sun's beams were frying them, to Mia it felt like they were just tickling her skin.

Burton, has it really been that long? Mia asked him. She waited for ghost Burton to reply, but he never materialized. *Maybe you think I don't need you anymore, but I do.*

Just enjoy the warmth of the coffee, and the sun, another voice inside of her implored. She couldn't decide if it was her own voice, or her therapist's.

Mindfulness. That was the key to healing, Mia had been told. So she focused on her breath as often as she could remember, paying attention to the feeling of different sensations: the wood of the balcony floor beneath her bare feet, for example. Or, earlier in the year, when she had finished Burton's last cigar. She used to loathe his smoking, but she missed the scent of his cigars sometimes now. When she had lit up his cigar, she kept track of how many drags she took, and acutely felt each breath in and then released it.

Now she sipped the coffee and savored its taste after each swallow. There was a colony of seagulls flying about in the sky overhead, and Mia listened to their sounds, studied their trajectory.

You can be as free as they are, she thought to herself. She had freedom from work. She had tried to go back to work a couple months after Burton had passed, but it had been too hard to concentrate. She'd messed up orders, moved too slow. *Still walking underwater.* Then when she had received Burton's life insurance money and had squared away their debts, Mia found she had more than enough to live on between that and their savings.

You can do anything you want. The trouble was, Mia had no idea what she might want to do. Maybe that was just situational depression talking. *It won't last forever.* Small pleasures, like the sun's warmth, made her believe that. If she could feel simple pleasures, perhaps she would be able to find great joy again one day.

Her best friend, Benjamin, encouraged her toward volunteering. "It's so easy to shut down and go inside of yourself when you go through something like this," he said. He had lost both of his parents when he was just in his early twenties. Mia had known him since college, and had seen how the grief had aged him. They'd met in their freshman year, and by their senior year he had lines in his face, which was also slimmer, and perpetual dark half-moons beneath his eyes.

Benjamin had been one of the few men in their class not to leer at Mia or hit on her: he was gay. Mia felt safe with him, so much so that they sometimes fell asleep together in her dorm room, holding each other in her bed. He was only a few months older than she was, but he was a big brother figure to Mia. He was tall and slim, in contrast to Mia, who was petite but curvy.

Benjamin volunteered once a month, serving food at a homeless shelter. "You should try it out," he told Mia. "We could really use more hands."

She agreed to go with him next time. When the day came, she felt self-conscious about how to dress, so she decided on a plain t-shirt, jeans, and her old pair of Converse sneakers that Burton had often teased her about: they were so civilian compared to all her designer heels. But Mia loved them. In her opinion, they were a classic that never went out of style.

When Benjamin picked her up in his Kia Soul, Mia climbed in on the passenger side and saw that Benjamin was frowning. He asked her if she was OK.

"Yeah," she started, searching his face for meaning. "Why?"

"I've never seen you without makeup, and with your hair back!" he gasped. She swatted him playfully and then buckled herself in.

"Hey, I'm going to serve food!" she protested. "They don't want all of this hair in their soup." She grabbed her ponytail and swung it toward him.

"Don't worry, princess, they'll give us hairnets, and you'll learn all the other basic tenets of how to become one of us common folk," Benjamin teased.

"Please! You're an accountant. I doubt that you've ever worked in any other kitchens," Mia shot back.

"That's not true," Benjamin defended himself, reminding her about the pizzeria he worked at during their sophomore year.

Mia rolled her eyes at him. "Does that even count as a kitchen? You made one food item!" They both chuckled.

They sank into a pleasant quiet moment and Mia watched the sun shine off the Puget Sound. Mia, thinking of Amelia's lips again, asked Benjamin, "Do you think that sexuality is fluid?"

He laughed in surprise. "Yeah. There have been times I've felt attracted to women, and other times I just don't notice them. I have always been attracted to men, so I feel like I'm definitely still more on that side of the spectrum. And then I had to figure out, 'well, what does it make me if

I'm mostly feeling attracted to nonbinary or trans people right now?' My romantic preference is for men, and that doesn't have to mean someone who was born a man or someone who is totally masculine. I think a lot of times, people can be attracted to all genders and gender-non-conforming people, but who they really want to settle down with sort of determines their preference."

Mia was silent while she took that in, let it marinate.

Benjamin added, "Then there are those who truly don't prefer one over the others: they fall in love with the person." He gave her a knowing smile and then turned his eyes back onto the road ahead of them.

After a couple months of volunteering at the homeless shelter, Mia felt stronger. Since she didn't have another job, she went there more often than Benjamin did. She started to make other friends. She loved Benjamin, and she was still close with her cousin, but she had isolated herself from everyone else for a while. It felt good to start letting other people in again.

The leaves were beginning to turn again, but the sun was still out late. Mia felt happy when it was cool in the daytime but there was a blue, cloudless sky above her. She walked along the road near her home that led to the neighborhood grocery store, and found a dark gold leaf that had fallen. She picked it up and turned it over and over again as she walked, turning over thoughts of her relationship with Amelia in her mind also. "Investigate your thoughts but do not judge them," her therapist had encouraged her.

Mia didn't know where to place it, how to compartmentalize it, the way Amelia seemed to. She was getting to see her somewhat regularly, whenever Amelia was in Seattle. They never went out to dinner together anymore, eager to get each other alone, but Amelia always slept at Mia's for at least one night when she was in town. Sometimes they met up somewhere in between, if the model was only going to be shooting in Tacoma or Olympia. Mia loved joining Amelia in the luxury hotel rooms that photographers picked out for her. One time, she had to convince Amelia to let her move them to a different hotel, as the one the photographer had chosen was not up to Mia's standards. "Certainly not good enough for you," Mia insisted, and Amelia grinned as she acquiesced.

But after several months of sleeping together, Mia had begun to feel like she needed more from Amelia. Yet she didn't want to scare her off. Amelia often referred to herself as a mess, and didn't seem to want to plan for anything beyond her next month's worth of shoots, and their next tryst. Perhaps Amelia worried that Mia wouldn't be ready, though. Mia wondered if that could be more of a factor. Maybe her lover was afraid to ask for more, while Mia was still healing.

I'm ready for you. Mia tried to send this message to Amelia psychically.

Did you get over me that fast? Burton teased, whispering into her ear from across their great divide.

"Hush," she rebuked him. "You know that I never will."

But as the one-year anniversary of Burton's car accident swiftly approached, Mia began to feel even more conflicted: she wanted to dwell in her thoughts on Burton, pay tribute to him at his grave on the anniversary of his death. But she also sensed that she was growing strong enough to move on to the next chapter of her life.

<u>October 14</u>

On the first anniversary of Burton's death, Benjamin drove Mia up to the funeral home and they wandered around the different plots, trying to remember exactly where he had been buried. Right after he had died, Mia had visited him quite often, but she had always fallen apart. Eventually she decided it wasn't the best place for her to frequent.

They drove around the outside of the funeral parlor and past many plots, until Mia recognized the stone that read *"Burton Hughes,"* followed by the date he had been born and the date that he had passed away, and an epitaph: *"a loving son and husband."* His parents and Mia had agreed on it.

"I'm not ready for this," Mia sighed, and Benjamin said nothing but surprised her by jumping out of the parked car and rushing to pop the trunk. Slowly, Mia got out of the passenger's side of his car, and followed Benjamin around to the back. To her surprise, she found that Benjamin had a bottle of vodka and a club soda and there was even a jar of cherries sitting in his trunk. "Sorry I don't have any limes," he said with a wry smile. Mia swatted his upper arm for teasing her. He made her a cocktail. "Do you want me to stay with you, or drive around and come back?"

"Oh, thank you, I'll be fine. I would love a minute alone with him, if you wouldn't mind driving back," she told him, and he nodded in agreement. Benjamin drove off and Mia went to sit before Burton's grave.

Sipping her vodka club and staring at Burton's headstone, grass touching the skin on her legs beneath her dress, threatening to poke into her stockings, Mia took out a napkin and a pen from her purse. She had hoped to write down everything she felt but the vodka and the grief both hit her hard and made her thoughts jumbled. *How can I condense everything I loved about you down to the size of a napkin, down to a haiku?* Mia wondered.

Did you come to say good-bye? Burton asked inside her mind. "No," she replied quietly but unwavering. "I will never leave you, Burton. But I think it's time for me to love again. To love more. That's all." Like magic, she could have sworn she felt Burton's lips kiss the top of her head, and he said to her, *Go on, kid. I know you won't forget me. I just want you to be happy. You deserve to find deeper human connections again.*

Mia felt relieved, and absolved of her sins of trespassing through Burton's personal artifacts. She felt forgiven by herself for having her thoughts of sex and romance with women. *Here I am, thirty-nine years old, and I get to find out who I am again. Who I am now.*

122

17. October 14
(earlier that day)

Cliff was blond and middle-aged. He wore the kind of glasses that appeared to have no frames, and his eyes darted nervously around the room when he got turned on. Amelia could tell when he was horny, because he also broke out in a light sweat and commented on her body a lot whenever the shoot was heating up. On a day like all their other days spent working together, Cliff went on and on about his projects, other models he had shot recently.

"I think my technique is getting better," Cliff droned on. "I am noticing better shading in the unedited pics. The proofs are getting easier to clean up in Photoshop." All that Amelia heard was *blah, blah, blah.*

"Have you seen Penni lately?" Amelia asked, referring to Emma by her porn star name. She always struggled for a moment internally, trying to remember if the photog knew Emma as Penni or Chloe, before she brought her up. Although Amelia had been eager to change the subject to Emma, she then realized that she still felt bored: she knew that the answer was always *yes.* Amelia and Emma basically just took turns shooting with all their regulars, when they weren't shooting together. She tuned in to the music she had put on her phone, which was pumping out of her Bluetooth speaker now: a dark, sexy, old favorite of hers, a band called Elysian Fields. The singer's hoarse voice was almost a whisper as she sang of sheets of night that were hiding herself and a lover.

"Yes," Cliff began animatedly. "We just shot pinup, but Penni said we could do real stuff next time."

Amelia forced a grin and tried not to let her disgust show. Cliff's thinning blond hair and weaselly smile, his weak spectacles and dad-bod made him unappealing to her. She knew Emma could fake her way through it, as she could feign interest in anyone, but Amelia didn't want to learn how to disconnect from her own body so completely. She resigned herself to continue working with Sam in Reno; she didn't find him attractive, but she also didn't feel repelled by him. He was kind, generous, and he wasn't imposing. She felt a peculiar fondness for him. Amelia had been seeing him once a month for the past year. She still felt that she needed to take some molly before every trip to Reno, and followed it up by having some whiskey on each flight. Amelia supposed that that was a bad sign, but she shrugged it off. It was steady money.

Touch me now, touch me, black acres are claiming me, Jennifer Charles, the lead singer of Elysian Fields, purred through the speaker. The piano keys danced but there was a reverb effect on them that made them sound as if they were under water. That sound, combined with the dark notes bowed on a violin, conjured up a sinister circus where one might find herself after drinking too much absinthe. A place where one might dance with Tom Waits. Amelia longed to run there, however nefarious it may be.

"Margot," Cliff started, "I don't suppose I could talk you into coming along to a shoot with Penni just to watch us? What do you think?"

Cliff's proposal caused Amelia's face to fall for a brief second. She perked herself back up quickly so that he wouldn't catch on. "Hmm, maybe. I'll talk with Penni."

"Oh, I already asked her. She wouldn't mind at all. And I'd pay you, of course," he clarified. "How much would you charge for something like that?"

Amelia didn't think any amount of money would make it worth her while, but she suggested a couple hundred, and he agreed exuberantly that the figure was reasonable.

She struggled to keep a sigh from escaping her lips, so tired of the routine. Cliff was a bona fide Guy with a Camera, and she had done the same dance with all of them: listening to their stories as they prattled on about everything else, and then finally they would cut to the chase one day. With Cliff, it had only taken a few gigs for him to come out and make his desires known. With other photographers, it could take a few years.

Amelia's plan of defense was to pretend she was interested but then decline another job when he texted her again. Or else she would pretend that she had some burly, new boyfriend who didn't appreciate it when she went all the way with another man, or even if she sat in the corner and watched while someone else fucked her friend.

She tried to change the subject to something tame, and began to tell Cliff about her last trip back East because she knew that he was from there and thought that it might entertain him. He stopped shooting, politely lowered his camera, and looked into her eyes for a second. Then his eyes began darting around the room again, until he focused his gaze on his watch.

Sorry, I forgot: the moving props are not supposed to talk, Amelia joked to herself. She gave up on the small talk and changed positions. She thought about the three hundred dollars that would shortly be in her hand after their three hours were up, and it made her smile. She said, "OK, ready: shoot."

Later that day, Terry's brush tickled Amelia's skin, the cold paint on its tip giving her goosebumps. It wasn't at all unpleasant. The horsehair slowly traveled down Amelia's leg as she stood with her arms at her sides.

She breathed in and out, slow and deep, her eyes closed, preparing herself for a prospective meditation.

The artist was quiet: he was in the zone, dragging his brush up and down Amelia's body before adding smaller flourishes to make spots on top of the solid parts. His silence enabled Amelia to fall into her trance. She tried not to focus on her body, but when she did, she somehow knew that it was beautiful. Having someone treating it nicely reinforced the feeling that her body was perfect. Suddenly it almost hurt to be standing still, having something done to her body that didn't make her feel like she wanted to run.

After an hour of quietly reflecting and getting painted, Amelia resolved to figure out some way to get her life together so she could make more true art and stop objectifying herself. She had no idea how she would make that shift, but she knew from wanting to cry over the soft strokes of the brush that were making her body feel respected and glorified that she only wanted to create—or aid in the process of making—meaningful art.

Terry took a large step back, carefully looked her up and down, and decided she was done. He nodded at her and then cocked his head toward the full-length mirror that he was standing near. Amelia took in the beauty of the patterns Terry had labored over, using her willing body as a canvas. She was a leopard now, and she drew her hands up to her face as if they had claws to display, and she let out a growl, feeling fierce and empowered. Then Terry shot photographs of her for two hours, silently concentrating on another craft of his. Amelia was internally processing her desire to change her situation, fix what was broken.

At the end of the shoot, Terry paid her one hundred and fifty dollars. It was the amount that they had agreed upon beforehand, but it abruptly sobered up Amelia from her hopeful fantasy, remembering how little the art world paid. *Fifty dollars an hour and only three hours of work.* She had no shoots planned for the next day, just hadn't happened to find any gigs. The week after she would fly to Reno again, where she would pick up another grand, which kept her from panicking about a light workweek. But she worried that she would be stuck doing sex work now, for a long time.

Or sit chained to an office desk chair for eight hours a day, for way less than fifty dollars an hour, she reminded herself.

"Why don't you just marry a rich guy?" Emma suggested later in a text message.

Amelia sighed. "I always figured we wouldn't have very much in common," she replied.

"Yeah, I always feel that way too," Emma agreed. "They're probably all douches."

Amelia had begun to feel she would wind up with a woman when she eventually settled down anyway. She had no preference for any gender sexually, but when she imagined herself growing old with someone, sitting up night after night, holding hands and cuddling in front of a TV screen, she pictured herself with her arms wrapped around a beautiful woman.

Lately that vision resembled Mia, but even as it made Amelia's heart flutter, it also frightened her deeply. She didn't know if the widow was ready for something more, and was afraid to ask. Amelia also didn't know if she, herself, could handle a full-time relationship yet. Amelia was all over the place, for work, still, geographically as well as emotionally. She supposed that Mia was probably a rich woman, or fairly well off. But she didn't feel their differences in class when they were together. *Definitely not a douche,* Amelia thought, making herself grin.

Your scent, like roses, your taste, like honey. How you touch me so softly, but with such confidence! You know my body. So many others had been too rough with their hands in the past. Amelia marveled at how Mia always handled her with such care. *Your skin is the smoothest I've ever touched. I miss your curves, want to caress each one again. I long to cup your beautiful breasts in my hands and bring my lips to your nipples again... I need to see you again soon,* Amelia thought.

That night she touched herself and allowed herself to imagine that Mia was in her bed. They would take turns pleasing each other and fall asleep in each other's arms afterwards. As Amelia drifted off to sleep in her bed alone, she found hope again.

18. October 21

Head pounding like a drum, eyes bleary, Amelia struggled to bring the woman in her bed into focus. *Mia!* Bits and pieces of the night before came dancing through her mind, the picture nebulous as if seen through a flimsy blindfold.

Mia had just shown up unexpectedly, but it had not been an unpleasant surprise. It was unlike Mia, but since Amelia had been missing her so much, she didn't question it; she merely grinned from ear to ear when she saw her on her doorstep. Amelia had planned to go to sleep early that night, and had already been tired when Mia had arrived, so she snorted some blow in her bathroom after letting Mia in. She knew that Mia wasn't into drugs at all, but Amelia wanted to be alert for her sudden visit.

That night, she had shunned all the concerns she normally would have had, if she had been in her right mind, about the next photoshoot she was scheduled to be at the following morning. Mia pulled a bottle of whiskey out of her large handbag and asked Amelia if she would like some. Amelia grabbed two glasses and Mia poured them each a couple of shots. They sat down on Amelia's shabby old couch.

"So what are you going to be shooting tomorrow?" Mia asked her.

"Pinup photos and masturbation videos," Amelia answered. She took a sip of Mia's whiskey, which was smooth. She shrugged. "Some guy Emma referred me to. I haven't worked with him before, but he asked me to meet for coffee last week. He bought me a cup and offered to reimburse me for my train ride, but I only had to walk there. He seemed nice, except..."

Mia moved a little closer to Amelia. She had grown to feel a little protective toward her lover. "Except what?"

Amelia sighed and shook her head a little. "He asked me if I would ride the train to meet him tomorrow, to the end of the line in Gresham, and offered to pick me up from there and take me to Sandy, where he lives. The train doesn't go there. He asked me, 'Are you sure you don't mind going that far?' I told him that I like taking the train because it gives me time to read books. He was like, 'Oh, you actually know how to read?!'"

"What an ass!" Mia exclaimed.

"He said it playfully but it was still kind of rude, right?"

"Absolutely," Mia agreed, taking Amelia under her arm. Amelia allowed herself to enjoy the feeling of being protected, but then she warned herself not to get used to that. Mia still lived in Seattle, after all, and Amelia, she thought to herself, was still a mess. *It's better to enjoy it when you can, without any expectations,* she told herself.

Amelia fell asleep in Mia's arms after they made love.

In the morning, letting Mia sleep in, Amelia scooped up some street clothes and scampered off to her bathroom to shower and dress. She had already packed the night before, had prepared what she and Emma referred to as a "red bag," which consisted of her lingerie, toys, makeup, and lube. She left a note for Mia and promised to send her her location on her phone, something she had often done before with friends when she would be shooting with someone new. Mia had informed her that she would be in town for a few days, and could easily check on her if she didn't hear from Amelia by a certain time, so the model agreed to text Mia when she was leaving the shoot to let her know that she had made it out all right. She asked Mia to lock the door from behind on her way out, in the note.

Amelia watched the buildings and cars go by as her train left the city. Her head still hurt but she knew that the aching would soon subside: she had done a little line before she left home, and had poured herself a cup of coffee in her travel mug on her way out the door, tucking the remnants of her small bag of cocaine in one of the pockets of her red bag. She negotiated with herself to only do another line or two if she started struggling at the shoot later.

Another voice in her mind whispered the questions she had been avoiding: *Isn't there always a reason to use?*

How long has it been since we've been sober?

Completely sober.

Amelia knew she had been drinking too much, but the drugs were reserved for special occasions: trysts with lovers, shoots where she needed a little extra help, nights out dancing with girlfriends, days when she was exceptionally tired, vacations…

Am I treating every day like a vacation?

There was a pure version of Amelia that she kept sheltered from Margot, and the guys with cameras, and some of her lovers: she was Amelia's inner child. Grown Amelia looked her younger self in the eyes, in their reflection in the window of the train, and promised then that she would get her shit together.

They couldn't go on like this. She wondered if someone stable like Mia could become a more permanent fixture in her life, if Amelia got healthy.

Both versions of Amelia smiled and liked this idea, and Margot didn't mind at all.

Amelia called Hank, the photographer, when she arrived at the last stop on the max train line. He described what he was wearing, and Amelia rolled her eyes, then explained patiently that it would be helpful to know what kind of car he was driving. Hank described an old truck and Amelia spotted it when it came around the corner. She threw her bag in the back and then climbed into the front seat.

The cab was hot, and the engine hummed obtrusively. The truck couldn't take turning or speeding up without some piece of it whining or trembling. Hank made small talk, and Amelia watched as they left the town of Gresham, and the countryside became more prevalent. Her stomach began to knot as the realization sank in that her phone might not get service, as they drove up a hill and onto what felt like a small mountain. They passed some deer, and the houses became farther and farther spaced from one another, until finally they pulled into Hank's driveway. She noticed that his house sat on a large pond.

There was an oversize shed next to his house, and a big RV parked in between. Hank informed her that his studio was inside the shed. Amelia quickly shared her location with Mia on her iPhone before she got out of the truck.

Amelia followed Hank as he plodded over to unlock the shed. He showed her the kitchen area, offered to make her a drink, and then took her back to the studio space. Amelia told him that she would love some coffee, and he took her to the dressing room first to show her some panties he had purchased for the occasion. Amelia tried not to flinch in disgust: all the underwear were full coverage, something a young girl or an old woman might wear. They were all in pastels or had flowers on them. There was nothing remotely sexy about them, in Amelia's opinion, but she knew she had not been hired for her creative input. She showed Hank what she had brought for wardrobe, and he picked out a pink and white gingham dress that looked very 1950s and asked her to put on some of his pink underpants as well.

After dressing quickly, Amelia drew another line for herself and snorted it hastily, a bit of dust escaping her nose. A crumb fell onto the vanity table and only then did she notice a pair of scissors, a box cutter, and a knife.

That's not OK! was all she could manage to say, and only inside of her mind. Amelia opened a drawer and swept all three items off the table, letting them fall into the drawer. Hank had gone to the kitchen area to make coffee. She struggled to hide her alarm and compose herself, as she figured that he had left these items out carelessly, not in order to scare her. She tapped the side of her phone to see if Mia had responded, only to find that she had lost cell reception.

When Hank returned, he apologized for how cold it was in the studio and offered to turn on the heat. Only then did she realize how cold she was, so she took him up on his offer. He said he was sorry again, explaining that the heat took a while to kick on. She took the coffee mug from his hand and had a sip, struggling not to cringe at how bitter the coffee was. It tasted re-heated to her, and reminded her of her grandmother, and her propensity to just turn an old pot back on. There was an overabundance of sugar in the coffee, and Amelia could tell that the creamer in it was synthetic powder. She asked Hank if he had Wi-Fi in the shed, and he grunted that it wasn't set up with that. Amelia tried not to let her fear usurp her ability to project sex, to get this over with.

They moved over to the set, where there were multiple lights arranged and a bed was pushed up against the backdrop. Hank instructed Amelia to walk around the area, put a leg up on the chair in front of the bed, and then sit on the chair, turning around to look at the camera. "Then climb up on the bed and stand on it, turn every once in a while, and pause when your butt is facing the camera. Then lie down on the bed and writhe around a little, and then we'll go from there," he said.

Amelia began to move around and attempted to replicate what he had described. After a while, she turned around to face the camera, curious as to why she hadn't heard any shutter clicks, and then realized that he was already shooting video. She didn't feel fully confident in what she was supposed to be doing. After lying down, she rolled over to face the camera again. She sat up and gave a little wink and then stood up, walked off camera. She turned to face Hank, waited for him to shut off the camera, and then looked at him with eyes that sought approval.

Hank told her that had been a great first take, and then he gave her the same directives for the next scene, ending his instructions again with, "And then we'll move on from there."

"OK, well, what am I supposed to be moving on to? Did you want me to go into the masturbation stuff next?" she asked.

"Well…" Hank paused. "We'll get to that, eventually. Just do more turning and pausing, let the camera take you in." Amelia did as she was told. She stopped and stood before the camera and grinned, as if she were proud to show off her granny panties.

Next Hank had Amelia begin the first masturbation scene. She felt so tired lying on the bed, coming down now from the coke, but she faked an Oscar-worthy orgasm. Hank marveled at it and said he was only disappointed in how quickly she had come. After reassuring him that she could do it again, he suggested that she give herself another right away. She balked and explained that she got sensitive after each time, and wondered if there was something else she could do in between the masturbation scenes. He asked her to lie back on the bed with her head toward the backdrop, and spread her legs, holding them wide open with her hands. Amelia lay back and assumed the position.

Stars swirled around her head as she became drowsy. She wondered if the coffee had roofies in it, or if it was simply the combination of having too much cocaine and not enough sleep that was getting to her. Neither of those possibilities sounded good, so Amelia tried not to panic and focused on trying to keep herself awake. She sat up and apologized, telling the photographer that it was hard for her to hold one pose for too long. He negotiated with her, asked her to get herself off one more time, and then do another spread-eagle pose, and then they could finish early. Amelia had been told that they would do four hours of work, and her internal clock said not nearly that much time had gone by, so she reasoned with herself that she had to take the deal.

Amelia remembered being with Mia the night before, and imagined being enveloped in her glow again. Allowing herself to relax enough without falling asleep, Amelia conjured up the excitement of a real tryst to keep herself going. She allowed herself to feel real pleasure, and her heartbeat sped up as she neared the climax. Hank and his shed were all obliterated and she was alone with Mia in some sacred space, for one moment.

After she came, Hank reminded her to hold open her legs and spread the lips of her vulva again. She did just that, although she was still not thrilled by the idea. He had her hold herself open for so long that all she could meditate on was the idea that she resembled a piece of meat, just lying there listless for the camera, her vagina gaping. She felt a swoon of fatigue come over her again, and the urge to close her eyes was suddenly too intoxicating: she gave in to it. *Maybe just for a moment…*

Amelia awoke to the feeling of her wrists being grabbed. "You see, I don't even have to use rope or cuffs," a deep voice said into her ear. "These hands are the strongest restraints you will ever feel."

Her vision was blurry, and she kept shutting her eyes very tight and opening them again, trying to clear them. The first thing that came into focus turned her blood cold: she saw that her captor was wearing a gimp mask. For some reason, she had always been terrified by the sight of them.

Perhaps she had had an ominous feeling, forewarning her of this very moment. She didn't understand the necessity, until she realized that he was filming again.

Hank was yelling now and demanding things from her, but she was so frightened that he might as well have been speaking another language.

"Wh-what was that, Hank?" she managed to choke out finally.

He removed one of his hands from her wrists and slapped her across the face. "Don't you dare call me by my fucking name!" Then the choking started. Amelia tried to yell until her vocal cords were too constricted and only a horrible choking sound came out. Then her vision swam and she didn't know how much longer she would last. But at last he took his hand off her neck. "You will address me only as 'Sir,'" he instructed her.

Amelia only nodded, wide-eyed and trying her best to convey that she was dead serious about obeying him.

Hank grabbed something lying nearby and began to beat Amelia with it. She had been hit on her buttocks with a crop before, or on her thighs, even her pussy, but it was much different when she was in the mood and asking a lover for it. Hank hit Amelia's breasts and she screamed, but he continued to beat them over and over. She began to cry as she kept screaming. "Aww, poor little girl. You know you can say the magic word, and make it stop, right?" Hank whispered in her ear.

"I…I don't know what it is," Amelia said through her tears.

"You know, baby: the safe word. There's always a safe word," he replied in a taunting voice. Amelia had no idea what word Hank might employ for a safe word. "Don't you wanna take a guess?"

Amelia thought long and hard as nervous, cold sweat dripped down her naked body. The only one she could come up with was her own. "Pinot?" she guessed, weakly.

Hank struck her again. "No, and this is what losers get…for… guessing…the wrong…answer!" he cried, hitting her again with each word.

Amelia shrieked in pain and called out for help. He slapped her again. Covering her mouth and bringing his mouth close to her ear from behind, he whispered, "There's no one near enough to hear you, little girl. You're all mine." Amelia suddenly sank back into darkness.

Her eyes wide open, Amelia struggled to find the light. Darting around fervently, her pupils couldn't seem to pick up any light or objects. Suddenly it dawned on her that she was wearing a blindfold.

"I see you moving that head of yours around, girl," Hank's voice came abruptly, a sinister whisper in her right ear. "You must be wondering what we are going to do next." She felt him back away from her. Then he asked, "Don't you want to know?"

Amelia tried to scream "No!" but her shouting was muffled; her mouth was gagged with something cloth. She wasn't sure if it was an old rag or a pair of those granny panties that she had modeled earlier.

That was the last conscious thought that she would remember having for a while, before her mind turned itself off. Amelia checked out. She was cold when she came back to reality again and heard nothing but silence. Her ears strained to pick up where he might be. She felt the need to urinate and wasn't sure what to do about it. Abruptly the room filled up with a clatter.

Hank must have been bringing food and drinks into the room on a tray, Amelia surmised, as her nose picked up the aromas of sustenance. How long had she been bound and subjected to his torture? Amelia didn't know, but she registered that her stomach felt empty, hungry, and that she was thirsty. She tried to remember how long a person could live without food and water, in case Hank was not going to serve her.

Her stomach curled up into a hard fist; food was sorely needed, but she recoiled with fear the closer the sounds and smells got to her. For a brief moment, she wondered if it was dinner time, or breakfast, or maybe not even the right time for a meal, but she would eat anything that was offered. *Pretty much anything,* she decided.

The bed sagged and Amelia knew Hank had sat down next to her. He asked her if she was hungry. Amelia merely nodded. "What do you say?" Hank asked her. She really didn't know what to say, nor could she speak clearly through the gag, so she remained silent.

Hank hit her face hard. It was jarring; her muscles tensed up, and her brain forced itself to focus, to try to send signals to her mouth to say whatever he wanted. Her ears listened hard, awaiting further instructions.

"The next time you disobey me, you cunt," Hank warned, "your punishment will be worse."

Amelia nodded to show that she understood. "Good," Hank went on. "I'm going to remove your blindfold first, then. I want you to be able to see what I've brought you." He removed it from her eyes as he had promised.

It took her a while to comprehend what she was seeing on Hank's tarnished silver tray; it was raw, porous-looking, pink and red. When she realized it was some animal's tongue, she swooned from the horror, and Hank hit her face a few times, just to ensure that she didn't faint.

"My sheep gave his life so that you could taste this delicacy!" he roared. "You best be grateful and eat it up, girl."

Amelia closed her mouth tight in protest. She didn't care if she starved to death now; she couldn't eat a sheep's tongue. But Hank grabbed her cheeks with one hand and pushed them together to force open her mouth. She managed to close it again, so he took one of his fingers and pried it open. Then with his other hand, he began to ram the raw sheep's tongue in. Amelia screamed until the tongue muffled her cries. Eventually she had no choice but to begin to chew; she would have choked otherwise.

It had been so long since Amelia had consumed any meat, but the taste of the sheep's tongue seemed to her a cross between ham and beef.

She threw up, involuntarily, as soon as she had finished swallowing the last bite. Hank made soft, cooing sounds as if he were trying to soothe a baby, and when she had finished vomiting, he brought a glass of water to her lips. Amelia drank all of it down.

Amelia's wrists and ankles were restrained with leather cuffs and chains, nothing she could break free from on her own, though she had struggled against them at times to see if she could, while Hank was out of the room. She settled herself when he returned.

Hank sat down on the bed near her and quietly began to uncuff her. Amelia was silently elated. When her wrists and ankles were free, he grabbed her body, threw it over his shoulder, and started toward the door. "We're going for a ride," he told her. The terror consumed her once more as Hank pushed open the door that separated the studio from the garage, then opened the trunk of his car, and dropped her in.

19. October 22

Mia hadn't known exactly where to start. She only knew that she felt pure terror after not hearing back from Amelia for hours after she was expecting her text. Somehow her fear informed her for the first time that what was at the root, for her, was love.

Her heart was a wide-open space in her chest, not aching with some longing to be filled by any available substance; her heart flopped around like a goldfish in a plastic bag, but only when she thought of Amelia. Her heart swam and dove, and looked for Amelia's hands to hold it.

I love you without knowing how, or when, or from where. I love you simply, without problems or pride: I love you in this way because I do not know any other way of loving but this. The verses of Pablo Nerudas's poem flowed through her when she thought about her crush.

Hungry as she was to talk with Amelia again, Mia still felt shy and clumsy. But she was also resigned: when she found Amelia safe, she would tell her then.

The roads were winding and narrow in Sandy, in contrast to how vast they were in the city. Mia pulled up to the house with the number that matched the address Amelia had sent her earlier in the day.

She spotted a beat-up old truck. She thought of how the truck was a symbol for masculinity, but how Burton, the man who exemplified, to her, all the brightest shining elements of being male, wouldn't have been caught dead driving such a monstrosity.

It struck her as funny how *masculine* could sound negative or positive, as she rolled the word around in her mind, sometimes tasting something bitter when she said it, thinking of toxic masculinity. When she thought of archetypal men in films, old movies she and Burton had enjoyed watching together in bed, she didn't mind the idea that a man was supposed to protect or be strong. But she supposed she felt that men were also nurturing, sensitive…real men, anyway. And she also liked her women strong.

There was Mia, being protective, nurturing, and strong all at once now. *I'm coming, Amelia,* she thought, without knowing what she should be looking out for, if she should be worried at all. Perhaps Amelia had simply forgotten to text Mia, or her phone had died. Still, she needed to make sure. She felt a wetness under her arms as she opened her car door and stepped out into the chilly air.

In the land of gods and monsters, I was an angel, living in the garden of evil… Amelia didn't know why that particular part of one of her favorite Lana Del Rey songs was stuck in her head on a loop. Her brain felt as if it was overheating in the warm trunk of Hank's other vehicle. If only she had been thrown into the back of his truck: she could have jumped out and ran. Just kept running.

A noxious odor was pervading the interior of the car, and the trunk was not impervious. Amelia had been locked inside for about two hours, or at least that was her best guess. She had tried to keep track of the turns, but it began to feel impossible to keep counting for so long. Her arms weren't tied anymore so she periodically slammed her hands up on the top of the trunk to see if she could manage to make it move. That began to feel like a hopeless endeavor as well. As Amelia felt the car stop suddenly, her heart also seemed to cease beating.

All she could do was wait in the dark.

The smell permeating the inside of the trunk was like murder. Amelia assumed, to her horror, that she must have been transported to some slaughterhouse town. Every muscle in her body tensed while she tried not to imagine what might happen next.

The trunk popped open with a loud creak to a dark sky littered with stars. Amelia noticed that first: the stark difference between this sky and that of the city. Next she saw Hank leaning over and only making two gestures to warn her: he put his index finger before his two lips first, and then dragged the same finger across his neck in a slashing motion second. Amelia nodded to signify that she understood. Hank slammed the trunk shut again.

Amelia started listening to Lana sing in her head again, as if she were praying to an angel of melancholy. *Save me.* After she had played the entire song in her head again, she felt Hank begin to drive some more, but only for about a minute. She waited for him to open the trunk again. She knew at least that much was coming.

Hank had parked behind a run-down motel, where he'd ostensibly rented a room. After he had popped the trunk again, he offered Amelia a hand, rather than picking her up, and she climbed out, desperate to be out of the trunk. He kept a fierce grip on her hand as he led her to the room.

After he unlocked the door with his other hand, he used his left hand to give her a shove inside. He quickly entered after her and pushed her down onto one of the beds. As he was digging through a bag of ropes with a bandana also sticking out of it, Amelia's eyes darted from him to the door, as she tried to assess how quickly she might be able to make a run for it.

Hank looked up and saw her deliberating. He grabbed a knife from inside the bag, brandished it wildly. Her face sunk in despair, which sent an unspoken message to Hank that she would acquiesce.

Amelia thought of one of her favorite guilty pleasures: true crime shows. She considered them a guilty pleasure because they were inherently exploitative, but she found forensic science so compelling. Amelia recalled an episode of one of the series she favored, but she couldn't remember which show it had been on. A girl had been kidnapped and tied up in a man's basement. The victim had been abused for several hours, maybe a full day or two, when finally she convinced her captor that she was beginning to enjoy what was happening. Amelia remembered how the perpetrator had untied her hands and legs so that she could touch him, and then after he was done, he had fallen asleep. Then the survivor had been able to make her escape.

That was the ray of hope Amelia finally found in that dingy motel room. Her eyes were open, the blindfold still off, and her mouth was still free of the gag. She knew she had to move quickly, in case he put those back on her. As her will to live continued to guide her, like a brave but bumbling toddler, she tried to turn on her charms as a means to distract him.

"We don't really need the restraints, do we?" she asked, trying to affect a warm, sexy tone.

Hank stared at her for a moment before his mouth slowly drew into a wide grin. "You bet your ass we do, sweetheart."

"I promise I won't fight back," she told him.

He shook his head and then stood up, ropes in hand, and walked closer to the bed, his shadow large and ominous behind him. That's when Amelia noticed that on the nightstand next to her, there sat a lamp with no shade on it, making Hank's face even uglier as he approached the harsh light.

Hank restrained her again, and she abruptly remembered the first stanza of a poem she'd read once: "Untie the legs and hands / tell him that it's over / no more of his demands." The poem and its format haunted her mind; it was a villanelle. She kept turning over the word inside her head: *villanelle*. The man in the poem was meant to be a lover but otherwise it fit; she had to find a way to extricate herself and put an end to all of this.

Somehow she slept that way: tied with her legs pried open. She sensed that she had slept a long time, and realized she had probably been sedated again, or was still feeling the effects of whatever had been hidden in the coffee. She awoke to the sound of Hank shuffling about the room, pouring liquid, setting objects on top of other things. She thought she smelled food and her stomach twisted with hunger pains. Her vision was obstructed by the blindfold again. She heard him stepping closer to her. The aroma of food turned foul as the unknown substance drew closer to her nostrils. Her heart raced while her mind tried to piece together the puzzle: what horror she might soon feast upon.

"Are you going to open your mouth nicely for me, like a good girl?" he asked her, a hint of warning behind his voice.

Amelia didn't resist. She thought to herself, *Fine. I'll eat dead animals. Garbage. Whatever it is.* She needed to survive. To her surprise, the piece of food he put in her mouth sort of crumbled and melted at the same time. It was creamy and tasted salty but sweet. Much sweeter than it smelled. And then she realized that it was cheese.

Astonished at how much she enjoyed consuming the animal product, Amelia left no room in her mind for guilt. It hadn't been her choice after all. There were paintings of beaches on the walls around her. Suddenly she realized it wasn't likely a slaughter of animals she had smelled on the drive in: it was the smell of a town that manufactured cheese. She'd bet anything that she was in Tillamook, but she kept that information to herself. She started making plans in her mind right away.

The idea of hitchhiking briefly crossed her mind, but then she decided she'd be too nervous riding in a car with another stranger. So Amelia settled on the idea that she would get herself into a safe, public area and beg strangers for money. After she came up with enough for a bus ticket, she would flee back to Portland.

Hank lifted a glass of wine to Amelia's lips. Her stomach recoiled at the suggestion of alcohol, but she had no way to stop it from flowing down her throat. It warmed her body instantly and she knew that, after having only eaten a bite of cheese in the past several hours, the alcohol was going to get her drunk pretty quickly.

Amelia begged Hank for another hunk of cheese. As the words escaped her mouth, they almost stunned her, but she knew that she would need to keep up her strength.

Laughing derisively, Hank fed her another piece of cheese. But as soon as she had finished chewing and swallowing, he made her guzzle down another mouthful of wine. Each time he forced the wine bottle between her lips, she felt as if she were drinking down a shot rather than a sip. She knew she would need a lot more cheese, or perhaps, if she were lucky, he might have other food to offer her. "Is there anything else to eat?" she asked him in a weak voice.

Standing and sighing, Hank walked over to a large paper bag, dug around inside of it, and came back with a baguette. *You've got to be kidding me.* Amelia wondered if this whole experience was tantamount to a date to him. *Romantic wine, bread and cheese platter. Were there grapes and chocolate in there, too?*

Amelia thought back to when she had last visited her favorite French bistro in Seattle, where she never allowed herself to eat more than a salad. She had missed the cheese boards and lusted after them when she visited after becoming vegan. *Maybe this will put me off them forever*, she thought.

Hank stuffed the tip of the baguette into her mouth suddenly. She chewed quickly to avoid suffocating.

Hank withdrew the loaf of bread and then pulled down her blindfold. He chugged some of the wine while he watched her. She was still working on the large bite of bread. Amelia's heart fluttered with relief when she saw him polish off the bottle himself. She had a slight buzz from the large swallows she'd taken, but she felt that she could function.

Rubbing her naked leg, Hank began telling Amelia what else he wanted to do with her. "Would you like it if I blindfolded you again, and invited some friends over? I'll let them take their turns on you, and you won't even know who is fucking you," he said softly.

Amelia couldn't even register the fear that she knew was behind the adrenaline coursing through her. She let it fuel her and propel her plan into motion. More visibly intoxicated now, Hank spoke more about the things he would have his friends do to Amelia, but she was so focused on her own survival that her loud heart beat drumming inside of her ears drowned out the details of his story. She heard a ticking in her head suddenly as if a clock were counting out the seconds until she could flee, but the alarm clock next to her, she knew, was silent. Having no idea what time it was again, day or night, Amelia didn't dare look at the clock out of fear that it would tip off her captor. She tried to move her hands along the parts of his body that were nearest, to convince him that she was a willing participant who wanted to be able to caress him.

Miraculously, he untied her hands. Amelia's heart pounded even faster. Who knew how long it had been since Hank, rancid and greasy with sweat on his body, had slept since kidnapping Amelia? She guessed that it had been at least two full days now. He was on top of her. She was vaguely aware that he was thrusting but she couldn't feel him anymore. Her mind drew a barrier between her and the photographer. She supposed that her mind had already been training for this, in a way: she had always been separating herself from the men she worked for. Now she only fought against the numbness to stay acutely aware of anything that might help or hinder her escape.

Amelia felt Hank drooping, his whole body slowing and coiling inwards, and she knew that he must have finished. Inhaling deep, long breaths, she managed to keep her heart calm enough for the drunk man to fall asleep on her chest. She felt excitement over this triumph for a brief moment, but she knew she would still need to wait quite some time to make sure that Hank was in a deep slumber before she attempted to disentangle herself.

The sweat from each of their bodies created a slick film on Amelia's chest that made her feel extremely repulsed. She didn't like anything connecting them, didn't feel comfortable with anything of his following her when she gently rolled him over to the empty side of the bed. Hank was snoring and Amelia had managed to nudge him so subtly that his breathing wasn't interrupted. Next she unwrapped the restraints that were still binding her ankles to the bed.

Padding through the room, her feet falling as softly as they could manage, Amelia crept into the bathroom. In her lizard brain, she had hoped to find a bathrobe hanging off the back of the door but this was no Red Lion. It was nothing like the fancy or even mid-level hotel rooms she had grown accustomed to staying in. She had no clothing to speak of: it had all ostensibly been left behind at Hank's house.

In her desperation to get out, Amelia wrapped a bath towel around her body and then hurried back into the main room. She noticed the extra bed, still made up with a blanket and sheets, and she was so grateful for that superfluous bed that she almost cried. After eschewing the towel, she grabbed the heavy blanket to adorn herself with instead. With no shoes of her own, and not knowing how far she would need to run across gravel roads or down unfamiliar sidewalks, Amelia was elated to find Hank's boots sitting by the door.

Now in a man's large shoes, with a thick comforter draped over her body, Amelia, who had no money or identification, quietly unlocked the front door. She held it still with her other hand before deftly pulling it towards herself so slowly that it didn't make a sound. Stealthily as a cat, she sneaked out, closing the door just as gently behind her. She emerged back into the parking lot and found that the sky was pitch black again, freckled with bright stars.

20. October 24

Mia examined her reflection as she touched up her makeup. She ran the smooth lip balm (which she preferred to Chapstick or gloss) over her lips. The flavor of pear and coconut was subtle but exquisite and made her feel slightly more awake. Her berry-colored lipstick went on next: it glided smoothly over the undercoat. Her lips were somewhat full, maybe a little smaller than they had been when she was younger, but certainly not tiny. She would have liked to have been born with a plump pout though. She thought maybe she was beginning to see tiny cracks in the skin around her mouth, but she couldn't tell for sure. She forced herself to smile, shut the mirror, and just sat.

She tried not to think about the signs of fatigue she had noticed around her eyes. She had awoken in her car and hadn't bothered with eye makeup that morning, but she knew that her exhaustion could be shrouded pretty easily. She had become adroit at covering her sorrows and worries with concealer.

Cars, vans, taxis, and bikes turned the corner constantly but none of them ever seemed to be delivering Amelia back home. Two days had passed since Mia had lost track of her. She hadn't known what else to do, after searching all over the outside of the property in Sandy (how she wanted to break in but was afraid of breaking and entering if Amelia had just been trying to ghost her). So she had settled on driving back to Amelia's and waiting for her there.

Parked in front of Amelia's apartment building, Mia clicked on the radio and heard the anguished voice of Billie Holliday. "*Good morning, heartache, you old gloomy sight,*" she crooned sadly. "*Stop haunting me now.*" *Indeed,* Mia thought.

The voice, like crumpled silk, tumbled out from the stereo, covering Mia like a comforter. She felt herself relax under the blanket of sound. *She'll come back soon,* Mia thought, and then she fingered a small pendant hanging from her neck. It was a smooth amethyst, hanging on a long silver chain: a necklace Burton had purchased for her. The last one he had ever bought for her, in fact.

Mia had never been a mystical person, but she wondered now about the significance of the stone. A quick Google search on her phone revealed that the gem was used for protection. Reading that made Mia feel like Burton was watching over her, and that all of this would end well.

The night air was cool to Amelia as she hurtled down the street. She sprinted past cars and houses that were all dark inside. Everyone in the beach town appeared to be sleeping and there weren't even streetlights to keep her company. Anxiously she jerked her head to look back every once in a while, to make sure that no one was following her, though she was certain she would hear car wheels on this quiet street and would notice the high beams painting the road.

There was an instinct she followed, as if tracing a scent: she hoped it would lead her to the main strip of town. If her luck was improving, maybe she would find a Walmart open. She wouldn't have set foot in one in her previous life, but she couldn't think of any other safe haven, knowing that nothing else in Tillamook was likely to be open.

In her mind's eye, she could see her bed in her little studio. She imagined lying down on it and sleeping for a long time. She could feel how it was as soft as a cloud and then she envisioned that the bed levitated and slowly floated out of her bedroom window. The two of them glided just under the clouds, and Amelia could see so much of Portland as they passed the old brick churches and playgrounds downtown. They flew over the big pink skyscraper and Voodoo Donuts. They kept drifting through the sky until they were in cow country. *Time to make the cheese,* she thought, as the darkness in the sky began to fade into light. She knew that morning must be approaching.

When she awoke from her daydream, she worried that perhaps she had been dosed with LSD or something similar. She didn't know if it was that or if she was hallucinating from the lack of sleep and food for God knows how many days.

She turned a corner and saw Walmart, shining like a mirage in a desert, didn't know whether to trust that vision or not. Amelia ran towards it anyway. As she neared the entrance, she suddenly felt dizzy and out of breath as the colors before her swirled like paint being rinsed from brushes and swirling down a drain. Then everything went dark as her head hit the cement.

○

"Oh gosh, hon, are you OK? Oh jeez!" Amelia heard a concerned, nasal voice before she regained her vision.

Someone else chimed in. She heard a deeper voice, masculine: "Are you OK, or…"

"Not," Amelia whispered. Some dark cloud was obfuscating her view, hiding the owners of these voices.

The woman's voice piped up again: "What happened to you?" she asked softly. Amelia stared blankly at her and took in the woman's appearance. She had round, hopeful eyes that were stained slightly with fear. Her skin was as white as sandwich bread and she had a multitude of freckles on her cheeks. The woman was younger than Amelia, just ripe for the world to pluck, and suddenly Amelia paradoxically felt more concerned for the woman before her than for herself.

The stranger wore the standard-issue blue Walmart vest with khaki pants. The man standing next to her donned the same duds. Amelia had always loathed the big-box store, but she felt relieved to see something familiar, as the rest of the world swirled around behind them. The air was cool and scents of the sea were wafting in, blended with that awful cow pasture smell.

"I don't know…" Amelia tried to say something that would explain her near-naked appearance and how she had collapsed in front of the store. "I … don't. Know."

"Ma'am," the young woman started. *Oh geez*, Amelia groaned internally. *No one likes to be called ma'am, do they?* But she found solace in the fact that she was still able to be annoyed by something that petty, something that was merely a pet peeve. "Where do you live?"

Amelia managed to explain that she was from Portland. The man and the woman looked at each other for a long time. "I can take you," the man finally offered.

Silence filled the air for a long minute, while Amelia trembled in fear, imagining sitting in a strange man's car all the way back home. Fortunately, before Amelia could protest, the woman jumped in. "No." Her voice was firm but her face was still sweet. "I'll take her."

The two Walmart employees had been finishing up the night shift when they had discovered Amelia. Meredith, the woman who was driving Amelia home, explained that she was just going to go home and feed her five cats, but she always left extra food out for them so she was sure that they would be all right for a few more hours. Nervously she chattered on, revealing the names of each of her cats, while Amelia sat in the passenger seat, with the motel blanket still draped around her. The heat was on and she felt grateful for the warmth and didn't mind the driver talking so much, even if Amelia didn't catch every word. She began to drift into a shallow sleep, and Meredith quieted down.

Amelia woke up gasping, and then immediately forgot what she had been dreaming about. She was distracted by suddenly needing to remember where she was, who she was with in the car. The woman behind the wheel smiled sympathetically and gently reminded Amelia of how they had met earlier that morning. Then she remembered that the woman's name was Meredith. Her face was nonthreatening with her freckles, flushed, doughy cheeks, and large, accepting eyes. Amelia relaxed, sunk a little in her seat. Meredith let her passenger know that they would reach Portland soon. "Do you need anything else?" she asked, taking her gaze off the road for just a moment, shyly looking Amelia directly in the eyes.

She merely shook her head and turned to stare out the window. There were strip malls and billboards: no more cow country. Meredith's soft voice broke Amelia's trance. "Do you want to talk about...what happened? I could help you make a police report," she offered.

Amelia's focus was still on the world outside the car. The vast, perilous world. Her eyes shook the way they sometimes did on molly: miniature eyeball spasms that caused her view to waver. She closed her eyes, hoping to make it stop. Opened her eyes to find the world still unsteady. "I can't," she said, her voice thin and apologetic. "I think he drugged me," she explained. "I just can't talk to cops right now. They scare me a little."

Meredith merely nodded and allowed a comfortable silence to envelop them both. When she arrived on Amelia's street, she tried one last time: "Whatever you want to do is fine," she told Amelia. "Anything that feels right to you is probably the way to go. But if there's anything I can do to help, please let me know."

She thought about it for a moment, her eyelids closing again so that she could concentrate. She simply couldn't imagine trying to make sense of all that had just transpired. How could she begin to put it all in order and say it out loud to someone? Shaking her head, she thanked Meredith, said that she just wanted to go in and sleep.

Meredith gave Amelia's hand a tiny squeeze, and then grabbed a piece of paper out of her bag. She found a pen and jotted down something in loopy handwriting, and then put the note in Amelia's palm. "If you ever need a witness or anything, call me." Meredith's eyes were solemn and Amelia could see that the woman was sincere in wanting to help her ameliorate the situation. She thanked her and got out of the car.

For a brief moment she panicked, realizing she had no purse on her, which meant she didn't have her keys to get in. The world spun around her as she stood on the sidewalk in front of her building, struggling to get her bearings. She bent down a little, put her hands on her knees.

Breathing in and out slowly, the thought came to her: she could ring her neighbor on the call box at the front door to the building. He would probably let her in. The old man was always cordial in the hallway, and seemed to be retired or on social security: he was always home during the day.

She turned toward the entrance, but something caught her eye and she stopped. Mia, sitting in a clean, white car, appeared to be waiting for something. Amelia trudged up to her vehicle, unsteady in her gait. Her heart pounded in her eardrums.

Mia sunk down in her seat, her face turning pale with guilt. She rolled down her window in anticipation.

"What are you doing here?" Amelia demanded.

Mia fumbled through her explanation. "I've been waiting for you, ever since I didn't hear back from you after the shoot. I went out to that place, in Sandy, but I couldn't find you. I'm so sorry!" She cried, seeing Amelia covered in a blanket, her hair and skin slick with sweat. "I didn't know what else to do! I looked all around the outside of his house and I looked into all of the windows and just couldn't find you. I didn't know if you were avoiding me or…" Her voice trailed off as she felt stupid, seeing that something dire had clearly happened.

Amelia could feel her eyes bulge but she couldn't think of what to say.

Mia looked down at her lap and nodded.

"You could've saved me," Amelia said slowly, realizing it as she spoke the words. "But you didn't find me."

"I'm sorry, I tried—" Mia started.

"Just go," Amelia shouted at Mia. Amelia thought she could hear her own angry voice bounce off the street, and then it echoed like a cacophony of crows cawing. Amelia ran up the steps to her door.

21.

Amelia felt as if she had awoken from a long hibernation. The slumber had not been peaceful; it had been more of a fitful sleep that she hadn't been able to rouse herself from. She was stuck in her bed, as if it were a cocoon, but she had no idea that she was evolving into a regal and fierce butterfly. The caterpillar she had been had rested and had eaten only the bare minimum needed to nourish herself while her joints all screamed out in pain from bed sores and trauma.

Eventually she moved herself to another room, in another building, where she showed a psychologist all her scars and let the hurt bleed out of her. The therapist was kind, with glowing skin that made her appear younger than she probably was. Kiara was her name, and only her eyes betrayed her age: they were deep pools of wisdom. She shined a true light of hope, one that Amelia had to follow from left to right with her eyes. Her counselor warned her that it would get worse before it got better, reliving the memories of the abduction every time she watched the light and traced its movements. EMDR, Kiara said it was called: Eye Movement Desensitization and Reprocessing. The exercise was meant to take the traumatic memories stored in the amygdala and put them back in order with the patient's left and right brain, Kiara had explained. It sounded like a hat trick, Amelia thought at first, but it was science-based.

Sometimes Amelia would ask Kiara for a more traditional talk therapy session instead. Her counselor's office was filled with orchids, and her furniture was made of bamboo. There were only lamps on whenever Amelia entered her office, with the kind of bulbs that provided a soft, warm glow. All of this, Amelia knew, was meant to soothe the patient. For the most part it worked: Amelia never felt anxious when she was there, but it was only before she went in each time that she would get nervous, knowing she would need to talk her way through those memories again.

When Amelia requested talk therapy, it was usually to process her guilt over not having made a police report. Kiara was shrewd: she knew how to talk to both sides of Amelia, as Amelia was torn about which direction to go in, and she knew to keep her personal opinion out of it as all good therapists are trained to do.

More often than not, where Amelia landed was: "I don't want to go to the police because I don't want to go to trial. I don't ever want to see his face or be in the same room with him ever again." She was also afraid that no one in law enforcement would believe her, that a judge wouldn't believe her, after they found out that she had been a sex worker and a drug user.

Finally on one occasion, Amelia asked her shrink what she thought she should do. Kiara breathed in as she weighed this decision, nodded her head as she composed her thoughts. Finally she spoke, in a comforting, compassionate tone of voice. "There is a part of me that hates to see him go unpunished. But a bigger part of me feels protective of you, and I have seen it happen, what you've talked about: I've seen women get ripped apart in court, and further traumatized, so I wouldn't fault you if you decided not to put yourself through that." Amelia nodded in agreement. So she was resigned that she would just keep coming back to this room until she had exorcised all the monstrous memories, and that is where she would focus all her energy.

Amelia's heart raced every time she reached the building where Kiara worked, anticipating that once she got inside the room, she would have to go back to Sandy, and then Tillamook. But every week she noticed that she was having fewer flashbacks after she returned home. She couldn't bear to model anymore, although she had tried to do a couple of shoots. At the last one, she had been oiled up with Emma, who had also had to whip Amelia's breasts with a riding crop, and the feel of the sharp slaps combined with the slick oil, which reminded her of her own sweat and terror, had made her feel too ill to consider going back for another gig.

Finally, after months of not working, having burnt through her savings, Amelia called her mother, desperate. She was one month behind on the rent and her landlord had taken pity on her, and hadn't posted an eviction notice yet, but had given her several verbal warnings that it was coming. She hadn't known what else to do. She had friends with "regular jobs," and she had heard of certain luxuries but did not have them in the world of modeling: there was no paid time off, no telecommuting.

Her mother was apologetic when she explained that she was barely keeping herself afloat. She had nothing to spare. Amelia masked her disappointment with an understanding tone of voice; she had never asked her mom for help, and she had always hoped that she would never have to. But her clandestine wish had also been, that if she did need help, her mother would come to the rescue. She drummed her fingernails for the rest of their conversation, making small talk but worrying silently about what she would do.

She continued to see Kiara. Her therapist would assess how she was feeling before each treatment, and then again after. Amelia rated her trauma response on a scale from one to ten each time. Her numbers got lower and lower. Although she reveled in the success, she still didn't know what she would do for money.

Eventually Amelia found her way into a job helping other survivors. Her experience working the front desk at the treatment center helped her get in. She had always been scrappy enough to sell herself for jobs that she wasn't technically qualified for but knew she was capable of doing. She found that hearing the stories of other survivors didn't trigger her own memories; she was focused on helping them through their own struggles. She didn't counsel them, but she listened, offered sympathy, and connected them with resources in the community. Amelia enjoyed the work, but she missed being a muse. She didn't miss sex work at all: she longed to do straightforward art modeling again.

Her rent and her bills were paid, though. Just barely. She counted her blessings every day that she had been able to not only keep herself afloat, but find an alternate source of income, and one that was rewarding, no less.

Amelia began to feel more and more like a pugilist each day that she got out of bed and swatted away every dark memory, and went to work to help people who were in less stable places than she was. She even took up kickboxing, and she frequented the gym when she wasn't at work or at Kiara's office.

Despite feeling incredibly fortunate to be graduating from EMDR, and to have a "square job" (as her model friends called it) without a college degree, Amelia ached for something more: she missed making art.

Her brooding over her lost profession came to an end when she received an offer from a photographer whom she felt she could still trust.

◗

July 13

Lila Fox was still as spry and nimble as her last name would imply; she darted around the room and caught Amelia from different angles. She was still calculating although swift. Amelia shook her head in disbelief so subtly that she hoped it had been imperceptible; she hadn't anticipated that her comeback would involve taking the train to Seattle to meet up with a photographer who used to pay her in nothing but exposure and compliments. Lila had been hired by a magazine up north that offered her a generous budget though, and Amelia had always admired her, and felt safe with her.

They worked all morning in a spacious loft in the Pike Place Market district. Amelia was naked and a little chilly, but so happy: she knew her nudity would show up on a glossy magazine page as tasteful, implied, and utterly artistic. She was posing for a print ad—her first time ever.

Amelia and Lila broke for lunch in the late afternoon; the vibe that neither of them had wanted to stop had been palpable, but Amelia's stomach had begun to rumble. Lila wouldn't have forgiven herself if she hadn't offered a break, she explained to her model, pulling snacks and drinks out of a large backpack. There were still so many things Lila herself couldn't eat, so Amelia knew that all the items offered would be safe for her own vegan diet. The two of them sat on the floor and ate gluten-free crackers, and Lila used a plastic knife to spread a nut-based cheese onto the crackers, while Amelia sipped kombucha.

As always, Lila was apologetic: she had just moved into this live/work space, she explained, and hadn't had time to go furniture shopping yet; she had just started shooting right away, working tirelessly on a lot of different projects. Most of them were assignments like this one, that involved capturing nude models in interesting poses while they stood like statues; hence, no furniture was needed for the gigs. "We could use a couch, or a kitchen table and some chairs right now. I'm so sorry," she exclaimed.

Amelia waved her hand at Lila as she swallowed a bite of cracker with almond cheese on it. She was so serene sitting there on the ground, enjoying a snack, watching the light fall through the floor-to-ceiling windows and painting the brown floor gold. The beige walls around them became bronze. She wished she could convey how excited she was, but all she could manage was a shy smile, as she told Lila, "I'm just glad to be here."

When they got back to work, Amelia's body barely registered the draft that had crept in, but Lila ran around, frantically looking for a space heater, saying again how sorry she was. "You don't have to be sorry: I hadn't even noticed that it was getting cold again," she told her photographer truthfully. "And you know… you shouldn't apologize so much: it's something I think we, as women, have been trained to do, apologize for everything. But you're so marvelous," Amelia added.

Lila stood, grinning, and quietly took that in. She nodded a little, and then swung her head toward the heater. "It should kick on any minute now." Then she began instructing her model in that familiar way that had always made Amelia feel as if she were on a Twister game sheet: *foot here, arm there, hand on that hip, other hip forward, and stick out your chin.* Amelia followed: as always, she had confidence in Lila, who knew her craft.

Amelia stood still, dreaming of how she might look like a statue of a goddess when she would see herself in print later.

After leaving Lila's loft, Amelia walked down Second Avenue. There was one more place Amelia needed to visit, one more person she needed to see. One last thing she needed to do. As if following her nose (or her heart), she turned left on Stewart without thinking about it, and then right on First Avenue. She sucked in her breath before she opened the door to Le Pichet. She knew she still couldn't eat anything on the menu, but she had earned a drink, she reasoned with herself.

Amelia hadn't been drinking as much as she did in her modeling days. She hadn't touched a hard drug since the incident with Hank either. Sometimes at night she smoked a little pot to help herself to sleep, but that was it. Her therapist had encouraged her to face everything sober, and Amelia was glad she had listened to Kiara; she could see now how it had sped up her recovery to avoid numbing her pain. Now that she had been doing so much better, she had started to allow herself to enjoy the occasional glass of wine again.

Sitting at the bar, she inspected the menu first and made her wine selection. Then she scanned the room, from right to left, until her eyes met a familiar gaze. The beautiful widow of another photographer she would still have allowed herself to trust, were he alive. Mia sat alone, nibbling on some cheese, half empty glass of white wine before her.

Amelia's eyebrows lifted when Mia's eyes met hers. Mia blushed, and then cocked her head suggestively, meaning to invite Amelia to her table.

Amelia scooped up her bag, marveling at its weight. She was always surprised by how much she needed to drag around with her when she traveled somewhere for a nude shoot, thinking that it should somehow be effortless: she should magically appear somewhere with a fresh face, no robe needed between sets, but alas the makeup and hair products and the robe were rarely provided by the photographer.

She plopped her hefty bag on the empty chair next to Mia and took the seat that was open across from her. The two of them sat in timid silence for a moment, until Mia broke the spell. "I'm so sorry about bef—"

Amelia interrupted. "It's OK. I know." A waiter approached them and Amelia put in her order, and then turned her attention back to Mia. "I … I'm not mad." Mia's eyebrows were the ones to raise next, questioningly. "I'm not mad *anymore*," Amelia clarified. Mia nodded. "You tried to find me. You had no way of knowing where he took me, or if I had ghosted you. I came out of it OK. I saved myself," she explained. "You tried. I'm uh…

I'm glad that you tried, and… I'm also glad that I was able to save myself. It was terrifying but…"

"It showed you your strength," Mia guessed. Amelia nodded.

They both sat quietly and contemplated the gravity of those words for a minute.

"Your hair looks nice," Mia told Amelia. Amelia tucked it behind one ear and smiled, and then thanked Mia. She had kept it black but was wearing it in a bob length now. People often told her that the cut and the natural wave in her hair gave her a flapper look, which Amelia loved. "Did you know that Burton always preferred it black?" she asked suddenly. Mia shook her head, said that she hadn't known that.

"Yeah, I actually originally went black last year in his honor, and since then it's just kind of stuck," Amelia explained.

"Well, it really suits you," Mia said, brushing back her own long, brown curls. Abruptly she blurted out: "I want to be with you, to take care of you. And let you take care of me. If … if you would have me."

Amelia was startled and she laughed, but not unkindly. "That all sounds wonderful, but I'm just not in a position where I could take care of someone, I don't think." She went on to tell Mia about how she'd somehow gotten herself into a job in a social services setting, but without a social work degree. "It's an honor to have that opportunity, but without the college degree, well, it pays about as well as an internship." Now it was Amelia's cheeks that were flushed.

She told Mia about the modeling she had done earlier that day, how nice it had been playing muse again after a long absence from the spotlight.

"I don't really know what else I'll do, but things are all right," Amelia asserted. "Things are getting better."

After a slow sip of chardonnay, Mia said softly that she was doing well. She still enjoyed volunteering, but she had the luxury of not working on days when she didn't feel up to it, or simply felt like chasing some other adventure. The insurance settlement had been ample. "I could support you. You could do only what you really want to do," Mia told Amelia, her eyes flashing in excitement. There was an energy about her that was dazzling, intoxicating to Amelia.

It was also a little frightening, as Amelia had cared for herself for so long, and hadn't relied on anyone else since childhood. Arms folded, she sat back a little, and asked Mia, "Why would you want to do that for me?"

"I haven't been able to stop thinking about you, ever since I first saw your pictures. Since I met you here." They both looked around the small bistro, which had a romantic glow with its soft lighting and intimate size. "This is where our story began," Mia added.

Amelia saw the face of love as she watched Mia watching her. Mia was ravishingly beautiful. Perhaps she could leave her old life, make a fresh start with this heavenly creature. Mia's eyes were hopeful and inviting as she waited for Amelia's response.

The thought of eschewing everything at that very moment was too much for Amelia. But perhaps she could make more trips to the area, and could invite Mia out on some real dates, instead of just meeting with her in hotel rooms. There was a warmth in her belly when she imagined that future: a combination of excitement and calm. The flame inside of her was steady. She took a sip of her own glass of wine, and said to Mia, "This is where our story begins."

Acknowledgments

Thanks to Andrea Bloom, Matthew Cornett, Abbey Pope, Aja and Alex Vice, Camille and Ash Perry, and Ilima Considine for everyday support. Thanks to my parents, Michael and Judy Fundahn, and my grandmother, Mildred Treherne, for always believing in me. Many thanks to all of my brothers-in-law and my other mother, Sharon Cornett, for always having my back as well. Big thanks to my little brother, Jacob Fundahn, and my son, Sebastien Cornett, for making me want to do my best.

Thanks to Matthew Feeley, Adam Nolen, Gary Waas, Nicholas Matta, LG, and Marcella Dean for being positive influences on my life and/or work. I have endless amounts of gratitude for the multitude of models who returned my requests for references when I was a traveling model. Thanks to Benjamin Coyle, Kevin Raybon, KaVon, Zheyna, and Kim Dralle for providing inspiration.

Thank you, Lynn McClenahan and Grace Cantor, for providing hope. Thanks to Peg Moran for the amazing initial editing, to Joshua Edward Wright for divine developmental editing, and to Jennifer Blackwell-Yale for copy-editing. Thanks to Steve, Amber, and Athen from When Words Count. Big thanks to Dave, Colin, Matt and Chris at Woodhall Press. Special thanks to Rebecca, Shawn and Alison, my WP sister authors, and to Barbara Newman, Julie Cadman, and Danielle Donohue-Liston for encouragement. And a big shout out to David Vaughn and Brian Becker for letting me take your baby all the way to the east coast twice while I was working on this baby!

I am eternally indebted to my friends who read, critiqued, and offered the most invaluable feedback. Thank you, Erin Kautza and Laura LeMoon for being my NaNo buddies last year, and to Jonathan "Doc" Ems for being my accountability buddy when I first started writing this novel. And the biggest thanks to Kim Neal, Jenny Feu, Rachel Chuganey, Olga Rudnitsky and Krista Nolen, who read every word and left no stone unturned in helping me find the flesh for these bones.

About the Author

Amy Bleu is a writer, musician, social worker, mother and retired model. Her previous work has appeared in magazines such as *BUST*, and in anthologies such as *Quarter Passed* and *Flatmancrooked's Slim Volume of Contemporary Poetics*. *In My Secret Life* is her first novel. Bleu is currently working on non-fiction and poetry. She lives in Portland, OR with her son and their cat.